CHRISTMAS CHARADE

When Nina Petrov meets charismatic businessman Fenton Hardwick on a transcontinental train to Chicago, she sees him as the solution to her recurring Christmas problem. Every year her matchmaking father produces a different hopelessly unsuitable man for her to marry. Nina decides she needs a temporary fiancé to get him off her case, and Fen seems the perfect candidate for the job — until she makes the mistake of trying to pay him for his help . . .

KAY GREGORY

CHRISTMAS CHARADE

Complete and Unabridged

LINFORD
Leicester

First published in Great Britain in 1994

First Linford Edition
published 2007

British Library CIP Data

Gregory, Kay
  Christmas charade.—Large print ed.—
  Linford romance library
  1. Love stories
  2. Large type books
  I. Title
  813.5′4 [F]

ISBN 978–1–84617–944–0

Published by
F. A. Thorpe (Publishing)
Anstey, Leicestershire

Set by Words & Graphics Ltd.
Anstey, Leicestershire
Printed and bound in Great Britain by
T. J. International Ltd., Padstow, Cornwall

This book is printed on acid-free paper

1

Nina hated flying. That was why, when the time came to arrange her annual Christmas pilgrimage to Chicago, she booked a compartment on the train.

She also hated being late, so that by the time she boarded Amtrak's silver-grey Empire Builder with its trademark red, white and blue stripes, she had had time to consume three almond-raisin chocolate bars, two brownies and the bag of fudge her roommate had given her in case she felt the need for a light snack.

Releasing a contented sigh after climbing the stairs to the train's upper level, she glanced round her compact cubicle of a bedroom. Yes, it was the same as always. Her own personal hideaway where she could prepare herself in peace and privacy for the stresses of the Petrov family Christmas that lay ahead.

With a speed born of familiarity, she shoved her suitcase under one of the comfortably wide seats that faced each other on either side of the window, and hung her coat in the narrow cupboard beside the door. After that, feeling mildly nauseated now, but deciding there was nothing to be gained from dwelling on the consequences of chocolate, she settled down to watch the remaining passengers bustle along the Seattle platform in search of seats.

Soon the bustling and scurrying tapered off and the train's engines began to throb to life. Any minute now, thought Nina, adjusting the pillow at her back.

A gleam of gold flashed against the window, and she stopped fidgeting to look for its source.

Farther down the platform, a late-comer in a dark grey pin-stripe was striding along the platform as if he owned it. It was the winter sun striking his watch that had caught her eye. He wasn't hurrying. It was as though he expected men and machines to wait for him.

Nina felt herself bristling automatically. If the time ever came when her father, Joseph Petrov III, condescended to board anything slower than a jet plane, she had no doubt he would walk with just the same sort of arrogance. And at the moment she didn't much want to think about her father. She would see him soon enough, and as surely as rabbits bred little rabbits, he would have yet another of his Christmas suitors lined up to court her. He had produced one every Christmas for the past five years — a succession of ambitious young yes-men who were only too anxious to acquire a pipeline to Joseph Petrov's money by marrying the only daughter he was determined to see safely settled down. Preferably with a brood of active children.

Nina had no intention of settling down. And if she ever married, which was by no means certain, her mate would be a man of her own choosing.

Forgetting for a moment that she was in full view of anyone passing by, Nina stuck her tongue out at the imaginary suitor and narrowed her eyes in a squint. At the same moment, the man who had given rise to her gloomy musings drew abreast of her window and stopped.

He took in the tongue and the squint, raised his eyebrows a fraction, and passed on.

Nina shrugged. If he thought she was making faces at him, so much the better. She wasn't interested in men who thought business was what life was all about — and that man had all the earmarks of a hot-shot tycoon.

She traced her finger down a flaw in the glass. He was attractive, though, in an unorthodox sort of way. It was his lips she had noticed at once. Unusual lips. Not wide, but full and alluring, surprisingly sensitive for a man who walked as if he thought he owned the world. He had nice hair, too, glossy brown and wavy. It matched the brown

4

of his eyes. Yet it was a strong face, and that cleft in his chin made him look tough and unyielding. He had the sort of face one would want on one's side in a fight. Funny, though . . . Nina frowned. It wasn't the sort of face one usually encountered on trains. Men like that were always in a hurry. Like her father.

'Ticket, please.' A brisk and smiling conductor pushed aside the curtain across her doorway, and Nina forgot about the man in the grey pinstripe and reached into her purse for her ticket. A few minutes later a wiry little porter arrived to explain the services of Amtrak. When she told him she had travelled this route many times before, he nodded and moved on to the next room.

Nina realized then that she had been so immersed in her thoughts that she hadn't noticed the train was already on its way. She closed her eyes and prepared to enjoy the peace of her own company until dinner.

That was as long as peace lasted.

When she arrived in the dining-car, the *maître d'* showed her to a seat beside the window. The man sitting across from her was the man in the grey pinstripe. Except that now he wasn't wearing his suit.

He had changed into a soft brown sweater on top of a cream silk shirt. Even so, Nina thought he looked noticeably formal for a train trip. It was probably his power shoulders, she decided. They just weren't made for casual. She herself was dressed in jeans and a loose orange shirt, and compared to him she felt small, frowzy and unbusinesslike. But then she wasn't businesslike. And she *was* small. Involuntarily her lips tipped up.

'That's better,' said the man opposite. 'Your smile is much prettier than your tongue.' He favoured her with a brief, appreciative appraisal.

Oh, lord. A Casanova. With a voice like gravel on velvet. Nina groaned inwardly. 'Thank you,' she said. 'That's a new slant to a well-used line, but I'm afraid I'm not susceptible to flattery. And we both know it isn't true, don't we?'

Just a flicker of annoyance crossed the man's face before his features smoothed out and he replied with easy urbanity, 'What isn't true?'

'That I'm pretty,' Nina snapped, resenting him for making her say it.

'Oh, I don't know.' He tilted his head and studied her with a bold, assessing stare that made her feel like a less-than-impressive heifer up for auction. 'Your hair is a nice light brown, and I like the way you style it — '

'I don't style it,' Nina interrupted. 'It just falls this way.'

A brief smile touched his lips and disappeared. 'Mmm. Straight to your shoulders and then up. I still like it. Your skin isn't bad, either. It goes with that orange tent you're wearing.'

She had known he wouldn't be able to resist getting back at her for that barb about his well-used line. She smiled coolly. 'Thank you again. I'm glad you like it. My shirt, I mean.'

'I don't, particularly. But I do like the shape of your face. Oval and pointed at the bottom. Reminds me of a nice fresh lemon. And your eyes are interesting. I can't make out if they're actually brown or green.'

'Beige,' said Nina through her teeth.

His lips twitched. 'You make yourself sound very dull. But you're not dull, are you, Ms . . . Do you have a name?'

'Most people do,' said Nina.

'Very true. Mine's Fenton Hardwick. Fen to my friends.' He extended a hand across the table. A tough, square hand that looked as though it had seen service beyond the boardroom. Was he only masquerading as a tycoon? Reluctantly, Nina gave him her hand, and immediately he wrapped his fingers around it in a grip that sent sparks shooting up her arm. She gasped and pulled away as if her skin had been scorched. Which, to her confusion, was exactly how it felt. She wondered if he

8

had felt it, too. If so, he gave no sign.

Nina hid her hand under the table as their waiter came up, efficiently balancing a tray of salads against the swaying of the train.

When he left again Fenton Hardwick said, 'Well?'

Nina sighed. 'My name's Nina Petrov.' There was no sense being coy about it. And he was unlikely to link her with Joseph. She didn't like being linked with her father. Once people knew she was the daughter of Joseph Petrov III, head of an industrial empire with tentacles that reached around the world, they tended to treat her differently. Though in this case that might not be a bad thing. She wouldn't mind being treated with respect by the smug but seductive Mr. Hardwick.

She lost out on both counts. He knew immediately who she was, and failed to show any sort of reverence.

'Ah,' he said. 'That explains it.'

'Explains what?' asked Nina, knowing she sounded crabby, and not caring.

'The chip on your shoulder, of course. Comes of being your father's daughter.' He took a healthy forkful of salad.

Nina put her own fork down with a clatter. 'I don't have a chip on my shoulder. And even if I had, what would being my father's daughter have to do with it?'

'It shouldn't have anything to do with it. But I've noticed that people who've never had to work for what they have tend to react like the spoiled little rich kids they are when one of the *hoi polloi* dares to ruffle their feathers. You ruffle very nicely, Miss Petrov.'

Nina opened her mouth, prepared to tell this obnoxious and objectionable man just what she thought of his totally erroneous interpretation of her character. But before she could deliver a blistering response, the *maître d'* had escorted another couple to their table — a man and a woman who gave them bright holiday smiles and began to comment on the menu. Nina bit her lip and tried to convince herself that she really didn't care what a nobody like Fenton Hardwick thought of Nina Petrov. Because even though he didn't act like a nobody, she refused to think of him as Somebody.

She ignored the small, nagging voice in her head that suggested she had brought at least some of Fenton's acid on herself. Not that it mattered. For all she knew, he was getting off the train at the next stop.

He wasn't.

When Nina made her way into the Sightseer Lounge later that evening with the intention of watching the movie, she saw that the ubiquitous Mr. Hardwick was there before her. But he wasn't watching either of the two small screens set up at either end of the car. Instead he sat sprawled in a brown leather armchair with his foot hooked over a narrow shelf running beneath the wrap-around-windows. He seemed totally absorbed by the darkness that hid the snow-covered mountains outside.

Nina made a face. All the seats by the closest screen were taken. Which meant she would have to pass by *that man* in order to reach the other end of the car. She hesitated, then squared her shoulders and stepped forward. He wasn't looking her way. And anyway she was damned if she meant to be intimidated by a rude, arrogant pseudo-tycoon who compared her face to a lemon and called her spoiled without the least justification.

He didn't move as she came up behind him. But just when she thought she was safely past, his hand closed over her wrist.

'Don't go away,' he said. 'I want to talk to you.'

Nina pulled out of his grasp, annoyed that his touch had made her jump. 'I don't want to talk to you,' she snapped, starting to move down the aisle.

He patted the empty seat beside him. 'Sit down.'

'I said I *don't* want to talk to you.'

'I heard you. Just the same, I'd like

you to sit down.'

'I came to watch the movie.'

'No doubt. But if you'd care to check, you'll find that all the good seats are occupied. This one isn't.' Again he patted the empty chair.

'I can't see the movie from here.'

'I know.' He smiled, a slow, curving smile that made her stomach roll over. 'So you'll just have to settle for me instead.' When Nina stiffened, he carried on blandly, 'And don't look at me as if I'd propositioned you. I don't go in for sex on public seats.'

Nina's mouth fell open, and she was so startled by his effrontery that when the train rocked suddenly, she forgot to maintain her balance and tumbled awkwardly on to his knee.

Fenton smiled again, with cool, suggestive mockery, and she noticed that one of his front teeth protruded slightly as if it had been knocked out of place in a fight. It made him look dangerous — and even more lethally attractive.

'Good girl,' he said, patting her hip now instead of the chair. 'Although it wasn't necessary to fall in with my wishes with *quite* so much enthusiasm.'

'Oh!' Nina struggled to stand up, at which point Fenton put his hands around her waist and without further ado deposited her on the vacant seat beside him. Nina felt its smoothness through her jeans. Quite different from the solid muscularity of his thighs. She swallowed, wishing she had the will to get up and return to her bedroom at once. But, curiously, she hadn't.

There was something very persuasive about Fenton Hardwick.

She sat as far away from him as she could, with her arms pressed into her sides and her hands clasped in her lap as she stared, tight-lipped, into the passing darkness.

'I owe you an apology.' Fenton's low voice rasped across her thoughts, startling her and making her turn towards him.

14

'What?' she said. Surely his kind of man never apologized.

'I said I owe you an apology. For calling you a spoiled little rich kid.'

'And a lemon,' said Nina without thinking.

He laughed softly. 'No, I won't apologize for that. It fits. Besides, I like lemons. I find their tartness adds a certain pleasing piquancy to most dishes.' His eyes left her in no doubt as to the kind of dish he had in mind.

All right, so the man liked a challenge. Well, she'd figured that. And the best way to make him leave her alone was not to provide it.

'I expect you were right,' she said distantly.

'Right?'

'I probably am a spoiled little rich kid.'

'Probably? Don't you know?'

He had the most irritating eyebrows. Heavy and much darker than his hair, with a habit of arching up in a way that couldn't fail to provoke.

'Not really,' she said, determined not

to let him see she was irritated. 'It's true my father is wealthy, of course, and while I was growing up I did have everything money could buy. The best clothes, the best schools, all my friends carefully selected for me. I'm an only child, you see.' She smiled, trying to make a joke of it. 'My father had no one else to keep in order.'

'Hmm. What about your mother?' Fenton appeared to be having trouble with his voice.

'My mother,' said Nina, stroking the hem of her shirt, 'is very beautiful. My father adores her. And she always pretends to do exactly as he says.'

'I see. And you don't?' The idea seemed to amuse him.

'Not always. He wanted me to go to some insipid finishing school in Europe. But I wouldn't. I made a stand and insisted on going to college.'

'Good for you. And did Daddy dutifully cover your expenses?'

Nina hated the mocking lift to his voice. 'He would have done. I wouldn't let him,' she said coldly.

His eyebrows did it again. 'Really? So how did you support yourself? A little flower arranging in your spare time? Or dancing lessons, perhaps?'

'I drove a forklift four evenings a week. In a building supply warehouse.' She didn't look at him, but fixed her gaze firmly on her own reflection in the glass. There were patches of indignant colour on her cheeks.

'Did you now? Well, I'm damned.'

'No doubt,' said Nina.

He made a sound that might have been a laugh. 'You give as good as you get, don't you, Miss Petrov? You must have led your father quite a dance. And my apology stands. I had no business calling you spoiled.'

'Why did you?' She tried to sound as though she didn't care but, oddly, she did.

'I'm not sure. There's something about you that keeps making me want to take you down a peg. Or two. You remind me of a woman I used to know.'

Oh. Was that what this was about? Some woman she resembled who had let him down? Whose assets he'd perhaps had his eye on? Nina felt a sudden stab of disappointment. She'd known enough of that kind in her time. Yet . . . Fen was so much more arrogant, more sure of himself than those executive hopefuls her father was always producing. More disturbingly attractive, too. Now if only . . .

No. There was no point even thinking about that. Nina gave herself a firm mental shake and, for something to say, asked, 'What about you? Were you spoiled?'

In the glass she saw his features suddenly go still. Then he stretched slowly, like a cat getting ready to move in on the kill.

But all he said was, 'No. I wasn't.'

It was all she would get out of him now. She could tell. In her line of work it didn't take long to spot the boundaries of communication. He'd said all he wanted to say, and so had she. There was no reason for her to stay any longer.

Why, then, was she making no effort to move? Was it because he was such a curious mass of contradictions? In some ways like her father, who expected lesser mortals to do his bidding. In other ways like a man who had little sympathy with the trappings of success. She wondered what he did for a living. And what he was doing on the train. But if she asked him, he might think she was interested in a — well, in a more than casual sense. Which, of course, she wasn't.

As a specimen of masculine psychology, though, she had to admit he was fascinating.

Just psychology, Nina? Not physiology? Who do you think you're kidding? muttered an irritating voice in her head.

'I must be going.' She stifled the voice ruthlessly and stood up.

'Must you? Why? Have I scared you off?'

'Of course not. I'm tired, that's all.'

'Hmm.' He tilted his head back and fixed her with a disturbingly speculative eye. The brown had gold flecks in it, she noted. Like the goldstone beads she sometimes wore.

'Sweet dreams then, Miss Petrov. Or may I call you Nina?'

'I can't stop you,' she replied ungraciously.

'No, you can't. And you may call me Fen.'

'I don't want to call you Fen, Mr. Hardwick.'

He shrugged. 'As you wish, Miss Lemon.'

Surprisingly, Nina felt the edges of her mouth curve up. 'Do you *always* have to have the last word?' she asked, but with none of her former acidity.

'Of course. I make a point of it.' He returned her smile lazily, and Nina was horrified to find herself wanting to reach out to run her fingers over those firm and deliciously promising lips — and over that seductive cleft in his chin . . .

'Good night,' she said, turning away quickly. 'We may not meet again, so enjoy the rest of your journey.'

'Oh, we'll meet again, never doubt it.' His low, amused voice followed her down the aisle as she made her way past the movie — it was something about two dogs and a cat — and hurried back to the security of her bedroom.

Much later — it must have been about three in the morning — she lay on the bunk which the porter had made of the two seats, and listened to the wheels of the train thundering over the tracks. They had already passed through the Cascade Mountains and were now gathering speed through the Columbia River Basin.

Usually Nina found she slept well on trains, lulled by the persistent rocking. But tonight it was different. Tonight she kept thinking of that extraordinarily annoying and objectionable hunk. He seemed to have a remarkable knack for getting under her skin as no man in her past had ever done. Not that there had been many men in her past, apart from her father's Christmas suitors. Who didn't count.

She heaved herself on to her side. There had been other dates, of course, over the years. Casual ones. Yet somehow she had managed to reach the ripe old age of twenty-seven without once having had her heart broken. Something of a record, she supposed. But then having Joseph Petrov for a father had made her a cautious player in the game of hearts, and she had no intention of being used as a rung up the ladder of some ambitious young executive's career.

The train slowed, shuddered to a stop, and she shifted restlessly on her bunk. *Was* Fenton — Fen — just another one of those? An ambitious young executive on the make? Maybe. Although he didn't seem to like her much, and if he was pursuing her with marriage in mind he was going about it in a very odd way.

Nina crumpled the sheet absently in her fingers. It didn't seem likely he was pursuing her at all. There was something determinedly unattached about Fen . . .

Hmm. She rubbed her ear as an idea, formless as yet, caught vaguely at the back of her mind. She made no attempt to give it shape or substance because she knew enough to recognize trouble when she saw it. And no way would she allow herself to become even briefly involved with that man. If she had to, she would avoid him by remaining in her compartment.

That idea lasted until morning, when the smell of freshly brewed coffee drove her in the direction of breakfast. And she needn't have worried. There was no sign of Fen. Either he had already eaten or he didn't plan to.

When she ventured into the lounge after breakfast and he wasn't there, either, Nina found herself relaxing for the first time since last night. Maybe, after all, he had left the train at

Whitefish or Spokane. She shook her hair back and settled down to feast her eyes on the icy splendour of the Rockies as they emerged in majestic white peaks through the clouds. It was a view she had never yet tired of — although today the clouds seemed unusually heavy.

After lunch, and with Idaho and the mountains left behind, the train pulled into Havre, Montana. By that time Nina felt quite safe in alighting with the other passengers to stretch her legs and breathe unconditioned air.

Immediately her interested gaze fell on the gleaming black bulk of an old steam engine — one of the last to run on the Great Northern Line, she learned as she studied the inscription. She was admiring its solid power, its connection with the history of the railroad, when she felt a brisk tap on her shoulder.

'You like engines?' Fen's voice, holding only the faintest trace of amusement.

Nina jumped. 'Yes,' she said, swinging round. 'As it happens, I do. Is there something wrong with that?'

'Not at all.' He brushed the back of his hand across his mouth. 'Don't be so defensive, Miss Lemon.'

'I'm not defensive.' Nina was irritated, and her heart seemed to be beating much too fast. 'And don't call me Miss Lemon.'

'Then you'll have to let me call you Nina, won't you?' He smiled smugly. 'And with a better grace than you've exhibited up to now.'

Nina sighed. 'How far are you travelling, Mr. Hardwick?' she asked pointedly.

'I'm not getting off at the next station, if that's what you're hoping.' When Nina glared at him, he added with a shrug. 'New York. If it matters.'

'It doesn't. Your destination is a matter of total irrelevance to me,' said Nina grandly.

It wasn't though. For some reason the winter sky seemed a little brighter and more challenging now that she knew Fen was still on the train. She decided it must be because his provocative presence added a perverse sort of spice to the long journey.

'Is it?' said Fen. 'Irrelevant. Then why did you ask?'

'I was merely making conversation.'

'I see. Well, come and make it in my bedroom. The train's getting ready to leave.'

'Mr. — Fen! I am *not* visiting your bedroom.'

'All right. We can argue in the lounge if you prefer it.'

'Why should we argue?'

His lips tipped up. 'It's what we do, isn't it?'

In spite of herself, Nina laughed. 'Yes, I suppose it is.'

He nodded. 'So we might as well do it in private.'

'No,' said Nina. 'We mightn't.'

Fen sighed. 'OK, have it your way. Come along to the lounge. I'll buy you a drink.'

Nina didn't particularly want a drink. All the same, a few minutes later she was seated beside Fen in one of the brown armchairs sipping doubtfully on a glass of pink wine.

'Why do you want to talk to me?' she asked, knowing she sounded unnecessarily belligerent.

'It may help to pass the time on this very tedious journey.'

'Why are you making it if it's so tedious?' Nina bristled at once. She didn't like people criticizing her beloved train.

'I hadn't much choice. Unless I was prepared to hurt my sister badly by throwing her well-intentioned gift back into her teeth.'

'You mean this trip was a gift? From your sister?'

What an odd sort of present to give a man like Fen.

'Mmm. She knew I planned to fly to New York on business right after Christmas. So she went out and bought me a train ticket. Then she arranged for me to spend Christmas with our second cousin, Addison, on Long Island.' He examined his hands. 'I have a feeling Addison wasn't altogether delighted. But it's not easy to say no to Christine. I should know.'

Nina glanced at him sharply. There was resignation and wry affection in his voice, but it still surprised her that anyone could make Fen do anything he didn't want to do.

'Why couldn't you spend Christmas with her?' she asked. 'With your own sister?'

'I'd have been excess baggage. She's off to Hawaii on her honeymoon. Which would have left me alone in the house we've shared for the past eight years. Frankly, I was looking forward to it. Christine isn't the most relaxing woman to be around.' He gave an exaggerated sigh. 'But she got it into her head I was working too hard, that I needed a rest. If necessary, an enforced one. Hence this damned train.'

Nina frowned. 'Couldn't you have explained you didn't need the ticket, that you'd rest at home — '

He propped a foot on the shelf below the window and twisted to face her. 'I wouldn't have,' he admitted wryly. 'Chris knows me too well. She also managed to get our doctor on her side. He's an old friend.'

'Even so, you could have — '

'No. I couldn't,' he snapped, obviously losing patience with objections he'd long since considered and rejected. 'Christine was genuinely worried. And I owe her too much to allow her to spend her honeymoon fretting about the little brother she brought up single-handed. At considerable cost to herself. So I accepted the damned ticket and here I am. Bored out of my tree and wishing I could somehow sprout wings.' He grinned suddenly, his ill-humour falling away like a snake's skin. 'That's why I expect you to keep me amused.'

'I haven't so far,' said Nina, wishing she didn't feel a certain sympathy for this energetic powerhouse of a man who had generously placed his own inclinations second to his sister's peace of mind. He might be arrogant and exasperating, but he did have his good points.

'You'd be surprised,' he said, picking up her hand and linking her fingers through his. 'I told you I like a little lemon in my life. You fill the bill nicely.'

Nina didn't know what to say to that, so she said nothing, instead staring out of the window at the snow-covered plains of Montana. Usually she found the sweeping white expanses soothing. But there was nothing soothing about the feel of Fen's hand holding hers. The opposite, in fact. She felt on edge, alive, waiting for something to happen. Something electric and maybe dangerous.

'What about you?' asked Fen, in that rough velvet voice that sent ripples up her spine. 'Why are *you* travelling on this lumbering anachronism?'

'Because I love it. I hate flying.'

'Scared?' It was just a question. She didn't think he was jeering.

'Yes,' she admitted, taking a quick sip

of her wine. 'I was in a very bad storm once. We nearly crashed. And I've always had trouble with my ears. So I only fly in emergencies. Which Christmas isn't.'

'No,' he agreed. 'It's an inconvenience, but hardly an emergency.'

She looked at him in surprise. 'Why do you say that? Don't you like Christmas?'

'Sure. It's good for business. It's also a time when people who don't have much of anything are made more aware of what they don't have than usual. You wouldn't know about that.'

'As a matter of fact I would,' said Nina, wondering why it was that just a few minutes of Fen's company was enough to make her want to break blunt instruments over his condescending head. She extricated her fingers and shoved her hand into the pocket of her jeans.

Fen's gaze skimmed over her with ill-concealed scepticism. 'Indeed?' he murmured. 'A time of peace and

31

goodwill, is it? I hadn't realized you were so full of Christmas spirit.'

'I used to be,' said Nina, more irritated by his sarcasm than she wanted him to guess. 'When I was younger. But now — well, I have to admit Christmas has become a bit of a — well, like you said. An inconvenience.'

'Oh? Why's that?' He smiled and leaned back in his chair.

OK, he'd asked for it. 'Because my father always has some tame apology for a man lined up to make sheep's eyes at me, that's why,' she said tartly. 'Some man he wants me to marry.'

'Is that so bad?'

He thought it was funny. She could tell from the way his lip angled up. 'Yes,' she said. 'It is. Because the men are always up-and-coming executives from one of his enterprises. He buys them for me, you see.' She'd meant to speak lightly, but couldn't conceal the frustration and resentment she had never entirely managed to overcome.

Fen didn't pretend he hadn't heard it. 'And that doesn't do a lot for your ego? I suppose it wouldn't. Why does he have to *buy* men for you?'

'He doesn't. I don't want them. But he's desperate to see me married and settled down. Preferably to someone in business. He understands business.'

'So I imagine.' Fen spoke drily and without noticeable sympathy. 'And why is it so urgent for you to marry? Does he think you're likely to run off with the milkman?'

'Not really. He's afraid I'll be corrupted by my job, come in contact with unsuitable people. Or come to some kind of harm. And he thinks that if I'm married I'll stop working and stay safely under the thumb of my husband.'

'Unlikely,' murmured Fen, contemplating the pugnacious angle of her chin. His eyes gleamed suddenly. 'Although it might be worth trying it. Just for the entertainment value.'

'What might?' asked Nina suspiciously.

'Keeping you under that thumb.'

'Forget it,' she snapped.

Fen grinned, satisfied that he'd succeeded in provoking her. 'What are you then?' he asked. 'A policewoman? A private eye? A journalist?'

She shook her head, refusing to look at him.

'Ah.' He clapped a hand to his forehead. 'I've got it. You test parachutes for a living.'

In spite of herself, Nina smiled. 'No,' she said. 'Nothing as exciting as that. I'm a social worker.'

2

Nina waited for Fen's eyebrows to rise. But instead they drew into a straight line and he said tersely, 'I should have guessed.'

'Why?' She stiffened at the sudden frost in his voice.

'Miss Cleethorpe.' He bit the name off like a curse. 'I said you reminded me of someone. I suppose it's a kind of aura that goes with the instinct to meddle.'

'Miss Cleethorpe?' Nina repeated, nettled by the implication that she meddled — or was connected to anybody's aura but her own. 'I don't know any Miss Cleethorpe.'

Fen gave a short laugh and pinned his gaze on the endless flat vistas of snow. 'No,' he agreed. 'But if you did, you'd get along famously. She was a lady I used to know well. Thanks to her,

I spent my childhood in the perpetual apprehension of being taken away from Christine and put in a home for impoverished delinquents. Not that I got into any more trouble than the rest of the kids in my neighbourhood. Trouble was just a way of life.'

'Oh,' said Nina, as the light began to dawn. 'You mean she was your case worker.'

'I believe that's what she called herself. We had other names for her.'

Nina tried to suppress her irritation. She was aware that criticism and resentment often came with her line of work, but that didn't make Fen's gibes any easier to take.

'Would you like to talk about it?' she asked, as years of training came to her rescue.

'Good grief! You even use the same jargon,' Fen groaned. He strummed his fingers on the arm of his chair and glared at a plane passing beneath a cloud.

Nina said nothing. Experience had

taught her that if people wanted to tell her what was eating them, they did so. Unwanted prying would only make Fen more determined to keep his feelings to himself.

It proved the right tactic. After a while he stopped glaring at the scenery long enough to turn his glare on her. Then gradually, as she met his look with disarming mildness, the harsh angles of his face took on a smoother, less hostile aspect and he said, 'No. I wouldn't much like to talk. But I suppose after that undeserved brickbat I owe you an explanation.'

'You don't owe me anything.' Nina gave him a small, cautious smile.

Fen swallowed a long draught of what she supposed was bourbon. 'True. But I can hardly expect you to entertain me unless I pull up my socks and behave like the gentleman I'm not.'

Was that mockery she heard in his voice? Or reluctant penitence?

Nina's smile grew more confident. 'All right,' she said. 'You can start by not calling me a meddler. It's something I try hard not to be. I know what it feels like to be constantly interfered with, which is why I prefer to give help where it's needed and then back off.'

'Is that what you're doing now?'

'What? Backing off?'

'Mmm.'

'I suppose so. If that's what you want.'

He grinned suddenly. 'I'm not at all sure it is. But then just for the record, Miss Cleethorpe wasn't nearly as pretty as you.'

Another come-on? Or was he just trying to mend fences? 'Wasn't she?' said Nina non-committally.

He shook his head. 'No. She wasn't. And I suppose it's even possible she meant well. But backing off wasn't in her character.' He paused, and when she said nothing he switched his gaze back to the snow. 'My mother left us after my father died. She said she had a right to a life of her own now that Christine was old enough to look after me. Not the easiest job in the world, so my dear sister frequently informed me.'

No, thought Nina. It wouldn't be. 'Do you mean your mother didn't come back? Ever?' she asked disbelievingly.

'Nope. To be fair, though, I think my father's death affected her mind. She used to write once in a while at first. Then the letters stopped. I had her checked out a few years back.'

No emotion. Just a bald statement of fact. Nina wondered how long it had taken him to learn to conceal his emotions so effectively — for the bewildered little boy to turn into this tough, hard-headed man.

'Is your mother still alive?' she asked.

'Oh, yes. Alive and living in Texas. In some sort of commune. She seems happy.'

'I see. And so you and Christine were left completely on your own.' The puzzle was beginning to fit together.

He nodded. 'Chris was seventeen when our mother went away. I was seven. And I'm told I kept her on her toes. Hence Miss Cleethorpe.' He shrugged dismissively, as if he felt he'd said more he should have. 'Don't look so stunned. We all survived. Even Cleethorpe. And I've managed to pay Chris back at least some of what I owe her. Thank God she's finally found a man who can give her the life she deserves.'

He spoke without inflection, but Nina wasn't deceived. The abandoned child had turned into a hard, determined man who didn't allow emotion to sway his actions.

But he loved his sister.

Nina had no idea what Fen did for a living, but there was no doubt in her mind that, like her father, and in spite of his brief flashes of humour, he would be ruthless in pursuit of his own goals. This was a man who had learned to take what he wanted from life.

But what *did* he want? For no particular reason, she shivered, and something, some fleeting thought she knew she'd had before, flickered like a shadow across her mind.

'And you?' she asked, carefully now. 'Are you — um — comfortably settled?'

'Shades of Miss Cleethorpe,' Fen muttered. And then, seeing her quick frown, he said, 'If by that you mean, do I have marriage in mind, the answer is no, I do not. I've never found the time to get to know a woman well enough to ask her.'

'Oh,' said Nina, not sure how to interpret the challenging gleam in his eye. 'All work and no play . . . ' She paused. 'You must lead a very dull life.'

Fen shook his head. 'That's what Christine says. She's wrong. I enjoy work. And when I've felt the need for other — shall we say, diversions I've managed to find like-minded ladies.' He put his head on one side and gave her a slow, provocative smile that made her glad she was sitting down when he added softly, 'I promise you it hasn't been dull.'

'I'm not a diversion,' said Nina quickly.

41

'I was afraid you weren't.' Fen heaved a sigh. 'I can see this is going to turn into a very long and boring journey.'

Oh! Of course. That was *it!* That was what she'd been trying not to remember. Nina stared into the pink liquid in her glass. Fen's dislike of trains, his reluctance to spend Christmas with his cousin . . .

The idea that she had refused to give credence to in the lonely, creaking hours of the night returned with a sudden insistence. She tried to push it away. But this time it wouldn't let go.

Yes, Fen might be casually on the make and much too autocratic for comfort, but he made her laugh when he wasn't making her want to hit him. And now that she understood something of his background, he didn't seem quite as obnoxious as she'd thought him at first.

It *was* possible. Wasn't it? He was all business, of course. That was as obvious as his pressed grey pinstripe. But from the little he'd said about his work, she didn't think he was a very prominent corporate cog.

He might be glad of free room and board and the chance to get out of spending Christmas with his cousin.

But — did she really have the nerve to suggest it? How was he likely to react? He might refuse and make her feel a fool. That would be — awkward. Worse than awkward. And yet — if she didn't ask him how would she ever know?

She stole a quick glance at his profile. His mouth was still curved in that soft, sensuous smile that set all her nerve ends on red alert. And for the first time, she observed a thin scar running from his hairline to just above his right eye. There were lines beside his mouth, too, that she hadn't noticed before.

What did she really know about this man? Was she just plain crazy? She had to be even to think what she was thinking. So why wouldn't the insanity go away?

Nina swallowed the rest of her wine

in a gulp. She might be crazy, but there was one very compelling reason for giving the matter serious reflection.

She would soon be in Chicago with her father. And Fen was a man supremely uninterested in marriage.

She put her glass down abruptly and stood up. 'I have to be going,' she said. 'Um — perhaps I'll see you later?'

Fen stretched his arms above his head and smiled lazily. 'Perhaps. I'm in Room A.'

Nina paused. Was he suggesting what she thought he was? She eyed his sprawled body with suspicion — and when she felt a quick, unwanted frisson of desire, she looked away. 'That's a deluxe bedroom,' she said, because it was the first response that came into her head.

Fen nodded. 'Yes, I'd noticed. Christine had sense enough to know that not even she could persuade me to spend two days cooped up in a box the size of a beer crate. Besides . . . ' He flicked a speck of dust off the fawn trousers stretched so smoothly across his thighs. 'She happens to be marrying the owner of an exceptionally large and successful shopping mall.'

Oh. So that was why he believed Christine's bridegroom would give her what she deserved. In Fen's mind success was probably what counted. Nina felt an odd flare of irritation. Then wondered why it mattered.

Without answering him, she turned to walk down the aisle — and promptly lurched against the back of a seat occupied by an elderly gentleman snoozing over his daily paper.

'Missed,' murmured Fen. 'Better luck next time.'

The elderly gentleman grunted, Nina frowned and Fen gave a low, gravelly chuckle.

Damn him. On second thoughts, maybe her brain-wave hadn't been so brilliant after all.

That evening she enjoyed a congenial dinner with three women heading for a convention. But when it was over, once again Nina found herself alone in her compartment contemplating a week spent dodging mistletoe and flabby, groping hands. There was no reason for the hands to be flabby. But they always were. She shuddered, and after a while got up and went into the lounge. No sign of Fen, so she stumbled down the curving stairs leading to the bar. It was filled with smoke. Nina peered through the haze, but no long body sat draped over any of the oblong tables, and most of the heads that turned her way were bald.

When Fen wasn't in any of the day coaches, either, Nina gave up and made her way back to the sleeping car. She hesitated briefly outside the door of Room A, then had a sudden vision of Fen's sexy smile — and of a predatory hand curling round the back of her neck, drawing her in, then closing the door softly behind her . . .

The porter, on his way to make up a bed, brushed against her arm. Nina started.

'You OK, miss?' he asked.

She realized then that she had been standing in the corridor with her eyes closed. 'Yes, I'm fine. Thank you.' She gave him a reassuring smile and hurried to her room to collect her sponge bag. Then she headed downstairs to have a shower in the small but efficiently appointed shower room.

When she came up again, demurely buttoned into a yellow brushed-cotton robe and with her hair hanging damply around her face, Fen was standing above her with his arms resting on the rail along the window. He had his back to her and seemed totally unaware of her presence.

Nina paused for a second, admiring the tight stretch of trousers across his rear, and almost at once he swung round. 'I thought I smelled powder and freshly showered woman,' he said softly. He looked her up and down. 'Mmm. Very proper. No breaching those defences, I suppose?'

'I should hope not.' Nina lifted her

chin. She hesitated for just a fraction of a second, then said quickly, and before she could change her mind, 'But I do have a proposition to make.'

'Good,' said Fen. 'I thought you'd never ask.' He held out his arms and leered down at her. 'I'm all yours.'

'Not that sort of proposition,' said Nina, suppressing an unexpected and enormously disconcerting urge to take him at his word.

Fen sighed. 'I thought it was too good to be true.' He jerked his head at the door of Room A. 'Never mind. Come in and tell me about it.'

'No, I — '

'You want us to go sit in the lounge car?' His warm brown gaze raked suggestively over her yellow robe.

'I could change.'

'Look,' said Fen, not troubling to hide his exasperation. 'If I had the slightest inclination to rip your clothes off, I could do it right here in the corridor, whether you were wearing that canary-coloured advertisement for chastity or not. So how about you put your lurid imagination on hold and come into my parlour like a good little fly. I have a number of vices, but attacking lemons isn't one of them. And to be honest, I find the suggestion that it might be most offensive.'

He was smiling, but his eyes weren't, and Nina had no doubt that he meant it.

'OK,' she said, taking a deep breath and making up her mind. 'Let's go.'

Fen rolled his eyes at the swaying ceiling and opened the door of Room A. As Nina ducked under his arm she smelled the faint scent of spice. It was a very male smell, ominously seductive. She turned to see him closing the door, and swallowed uncomfortably.

Fen's bunk had not yet been pulled out for the night, and Nina took in at once that his room was more than big enough for two people. It was fitted with a sofa and chair and a pull-out table, and he also had his own bathroom and sink. If her mind hadn't been on another, more pressing matter, she might have regretted her annual refusal to let her father buy her ticket. Joseph would have settled for nothing less than this.

'Have a seat,' said Fen.

She took the chair, then wished she hadn't, because Fen immediately propped a pillow behind his head and swung his legs up on to the sofa. He looked disturbingly alluring stretched out like that — lean, intimate and altogether too available.

'Well?' he said, smiling like a predatory cat. 'What is it you want to propose? I'm open to offers.'

Yes, she had no doubt he was. In more ways than one. And that, of course, was precisely why she was here. It was also why she seemed to be having trouble finding words.

'It's not what you're thinking,' she blurted, nervously checking the top button on her robe. 'You see, what I need — well, want, anyway — is a man.' No, that hadn't come out right. 'Just for

Christmas,' she explained, making it worse.

Fen stretched, more catlike than ever, and his goldstone eyes gleamed at her in the light beaming down from the lamp above his head. 'Interesting. I've never been gift-wrapped before. But I guess I could go for it.'

'No, you don't understand.' Nina put her hands up to her cheeks to hide a blush. 'I meant I need someone to pretend to be a man — '

'Pretend? Now look here, Miss Lemon, I've been accused of many things in my time, but I'll have you know — '

'Stop it,' she said, exasperation overcoming her nervousness. 'Please — just listen.'

'I'm all ears,' he replied, linking his hands behind his head.

He wasn't. He was all sinew and muscle and endless leg, and his lips were . . . No. Oh, no! Nina pushed herself up straight and took a long, deliberate breath.

Fen ran a careless hand through his hair and closed his eyes.

'Fen,' she said desperately, 'I can't talk to you if you're going to go to sleep.'

He opened his eyes at once, and she wished he hadn't, because they sent her a message so explicit it brought goose bumps to her skin. 'Who says I'm sleeping?' he said.

Nina shook her head. 'You don't understand. The point is — is that I need someone to pretend to be the man in my life.' Oh God! That had come out as if she were asking for a second cup of tea. She tried again. 'Someone who will convince my father to lay off the troops and — and who will go away once the holiday is over. Do you see what I mean?'

'Not really. Wouldn't it be easier, and a lot more honest, just to go along with the troops?' Fen's lazy drawl immediately set her teeth on edge.

'No. No, it wouldn't.' She curled her fingers tightly in her lap. 'Dad picks them for their persistence. The last three followed me to Seattle. *After* they'd spent the entire Christmas week breathing down my neck, dragging me under the mistletoe, and making sheep's eyes at me over the leftover turkey.'

Fen appeared to have something caught in his throat.

'Well,' she asked doubtfully, when she had his attention again. 'Will you do it?'

'What? Make sheep's eyes at you over the turkey?'

Nina gritted her bicuspids. 'No. Be my man of the moment. You — you're rude and impossible. But at least you don't smell of martinis.' When he only gazed at her in what appeared to be total disbelief, she added hurriedly, 'And once the holiday season is over I know you won't ask me to marry you.'

'Mmm. On that you *can* trust me,' agreed Fen. 'I may be rude and impossible, but I've yet to propose to a lemon.'

'So you'll do it?' Nina kept her temper with an effort.

'No. I will not.' He switched off the light above his head, throwing his face into shadowed relief.

He'd turned her down. She'd found the courage to ask him, and he'd turned her down. 'But why not?' she persisted. There was nothing to be gained from giving up now. She had already made herself look ridiculous. 'You don't want to spend Christmas in New York. You said you didn't.'

'I don't much. Nor do I want to spend it in Chicago pretending to be someone I'm not.'

'You don't have to be someone you're not. You can be you. My father won't know you. Will he?'

'I doubt it.'

That was all right then. At least . . .

'Fen — what is it that you actually do?' It probably didn't matter, but just in case she could get him to change his mind, she ought to know that much about him.

'I'm in imported food.' Fen didn't elaborate.

Oh, so he was just a buyer for some fancy food company. That explained the trip to New York. And as food wasn't one of her father's sidelines, there wouldn't be much danger of his knowing more about Fen than he should. Her plan *could* work — if he'd only co-operate.

'Fen,' she said, 'I'm certain there won't be a problem with food — '

'None at all. Because I'm not falling in with your little scheme.'

He spoke pleasantly enough, but he was adamant. She recognized that uncompromising tone. She'd heard it often enough from Joseph. But . . . She held her breath for a moment. What Joseph couldn't demand, he bought.

Nina shut her eyes. She didn't want to *buy* Fen's co-operation. Besides, she wasn't sure he could be bought. But if he could — if he could, she supposed he would be better than the alternative, which would be to spend yet another Christmas dodging moist lips, groping hands and phony protestations of adoration.

Joseph had always told her everyone had his price.

She made up her mind. 'I'll make it worth your while,' she said quickly, before she could change it again. 'How much will it take?'

She heard his indrawn breath, saw the sudden rigidity of his shoulders, and for a moment she thought — hoped? — he would refuse. But after a lengthy silence during which she could almost hear the wheels grinding in his brain, he said in a crisp, businesslike voice that held not the slightest hint of velvet, 'That depends. How much are you offering, Miss Petrov? And precisely what will you expect in return?' There was a glint in his eye that Nina didn't know quite how to take.

She gulped. Why was he responding with such detachment? And he had called her Miss Petrov again, the name he associated with undeserved wealth and privilege. Yet he was apparently ready to strike a bargain. She felt a vague stab of unease.

'I told you,' she said, checking her top button again. 'I — well, I just want you to be my man for a few days.'

'Yes? And exactly what services does the job entail?' He raised his arms above his head and flexed his shoulders against the pillow. 'I've never been paid for my favours before.'

Nina gulped. She couldn't take her eyes off him. And she was almost sure he knew it, and was greatly enjoying her reluctant fascination.

But he sounded about as warm as an iceberg. Did he really think she was the kind of woman who would pay a man to — to . . . Well, yes. Obviously he did. She swallowed. Maybe this hadn't been such a great idea after all. Surely there was still time to back out . . .

'How much?' asked Fen, before she could put her thoughts into words. And was that minuscule movement of his lips actually a quickly suppressed smile?

No, it couldn't be. 'I — don't know,' she mumbled, biting the inside of her

cheek. 'I didn't mean I expected you to
— um — '

'Make love to you? Well, that lowers
the price then, doesn't it?'

Oh, God. This was worse than she
could possibly have imagined. And now
she was so confused that she didn't
know *how* to back out.

She moistened her lips. 'How much
do you want?'

He named a figure. It wasn't
exorbitant. Well within her means. And
if Fenton Hardwick thought it was
enough, he must be even further down
the corporate ladder than she'd imagined. Still, he didn't *seem* to see her
relationship to her father as a ticket to
his personal advancement. That was
something. Better than Joseph's tame
suitors.

'Yes,' she agreed. 'Yes, all right. I'll
get my cheque book.' She stood up, and
beneath her the wheels of the train kept
pace with the uneven pounding of her
heart.

A few minutes later, with a few quick

strokes of her pen, the deed was done.

Fen inspected the cheque she had handed him then gave her a curt nod. 'Seems in order,' he drawled.

'Good.' Nina bit her lip. 'Um — we'll be in Chicago tomorrow night, so do you think we'd better — '

'Practice our Christmas charade?' he suggested, removing a hair from her shoulder, studying it, then flicking it on to the floor.

'Well — make sure we both tell the same story, at least,' amended Nina, feeling numb.

He nodded. 'Sounds advisable. We'll meet for breakfast, shall we? Good night, Miss Petrov.'

'Good night.' She waited, wondering if he would try to take advantage of their altered relationship. But all he did was reach for the bell to call the porter to make up his bed.

Nina looked back once before she left. Fen was draped across the sofa looking relaxed and sexy. And just before she slid the door shut, she saw him push a hand through his hair. When he lowered it, she caught a glimpse of his eyes. They were lit with a dark, devilish glitter that made her wonder what she had let herself in for.

She shook her head, paused for a moment, then made her way to her compartment feeling much the same as she had felt as a child on the day she learned that Santa Claus was a myth. Which didn't make a whole lot of sense.

You're being a fool, Nina Petrov, she lectured herself as she collapsed on top of her bed. You've got what you asked for. A man to take the heat off over Christmas — a man who won't try to kiss you in corners and who has no intention of remaining in your life.

Except, murmured that tiresome little voice in her head, that being kissed in corners by Fen Hardwick might be an experience that . . . No. She wasn't even going to allow herself to think it. She had bought Fen, just as her father had bought all the others. And the fact that he could be attractive and amusing when it suited him didn't make him any different from the rest. He was a man. He could be bought. Once he'd done his job he'd be gone. For good. Unexpectedly a lump began to form in her throat. She swallowed, twice, and it went away.

Good. Now, with luck, she would have a peaceful Christmas. And for once when she returned to Seattle there would be no scheming swain in hot pursuit.

Nina settled her head on the pillow and closed her eyes, hoping these bracing reflections would lead to an undisturbed night. But sleep didn't come easily, and by the time she slouched into breakfast the following morning she felt a lot like a soufflé that hadn't happened. Not that soufflés felt anything much, she supposed. She wished *she* didn't. Because there was Fen, already seated at a table, and with his white smile and slightly damp skin, he looked like a gift to womankind from the god of mornings.

'Good grief! The lemon's turned into a lime,' he exclaimed, standing up as soon as he saw her come in. Once she was seated he sat down again and studied her more closely. 'Do you realize your skin has turned green?'

'Thanks,' said Nina sourly. 'I had a bad night, all right?'

'I can see that.' He eyed her shrewdly. 'Having second thoughts?'

'No. Are you? You can return my cheque if you want to.' She held her breath, not sure what she was hoping for but knowing his answer was important.

Fen's eyes glinted with sudden malice. 'Why should I? We struck a bargain. I haven't much use for people who break their promises.'

'In other words you do what you've been paid to do,' Nina said flatly. 'I suppose I ought to respect that.'

'I suppose you ought — since Daddy's money puts you in the fortunate position of being able to buy whatever, and whoever, you want.'

'I thought money was what you wanted,' said Nina dully, resenting enormously the fact that there was some truth to what he said — even though she hadn't accepted help from Joseph for many years. 'And it's not my father's money. It's mine.' She paused while the waiter took her order, then muttered, 'This isn't going to work, is it?'

'Oh, yes, it is,' said Fen. 'You're not getting off that easily, my girl.'

'So you do want the money?'

Fen didn't answer directly. Instead he peeled the foil back from a small square package and began to spread jam on his toast. 'What do you think?' he asked.

'Well — you took it.'

'And you offered it.'

His voice was smooth, unemotional. But he *had* taken the money, so she couldn't have made a mistake. 'Yes,' she said, making a decision. 'I did. So I guess we'll just have to make it work.'

'Oh, it'll work,' said Fen. 'I'll see to it.'

She didn't like the sound of that. The edge was back in his voice, and she had a feeling that although he would keep his side of the bargain, he didn't intend to make it easy.

She was right. The train, which was running a little late, was just pulling into St. Paul, Minnesota, when Fen threw down his napkin and said, 'Come on. We'd better start as we mean to go on. Let the world get a good look at the young lovers — just in case Daddy's spies are on the prowl.'

'They won't be. And I haven't finished my coffee — '

'Then finish it. We'll be in the station in a minute.'

Nina decided the matter wasn't worth arguing about, so she swallowed her coffee and made her way to her compartment to fetch her coat. When Fen met her at the door he took her arm in a proprietorial fashion and marched her briskly out on to the platform.

'Brr. It's cold,' said Nina, making conversation to take her mind off his disturbing proximity.

'Not as balmy as Seattle,' he conceded. 'And I suppose that as the besotted and attentive suitor it's up to me to keep you warm.'

Before Nina could tell him that wasn't necessary, he had looped an arm over her shoulder and tucked her up against his side. Then he began to whisk her along the platform towards the station. 'Better?'

It was. Much better. And much too warm. She could feel the lean length of him all along her side. 'Yes.' She cleared her throat nervously. 'Yes. Thank you. I'm fine now. You don't have to hold me.'

'Maybe I like holding you,' he said amiably. Too amiably.

'Oh.' She threw him a doubtful glance as they made their way through the glass doors leading into the crowded station. 'But you can't. It's not part of the bargain.'

'What isn't? Holding or liking?'

Nina didn't answer, mainly because she couldn't think of anything to say.

Holding her probably *was* part of the bargain if they were to convince Joseph they were seriously devoted.

Fen had just steered her round a crowd of noisy teenagers surrounding a mountain of packsacks when they almost collided with a harried young mother in pursuit of giggling twin boys. The boys were running determinedly for the exit. 'Roddy,' the distracted mother was shouting. 'Reggie! If you don't come back right this minute, I'll — '

'Allow me,' said Fen. To Nina's immense relief, he released her and strode purposefully after the two offenders. Within seconds he had scooped them up, one squirming little body under each arm. 'Where would you like them?' he asked the mother as she came panting up behind him.

'In a cage,' she groaned. 'But I guess you better put them over there.' She pointed at the nearest row of chairs.

Fen nodded and sat the boys down. 'And no more of your nonsense,' he told them sternly. 'Give your mother one more bit of trouble before she gets you safely on the train and you'll have me to answer to. Understand?'

They nodded mutely, two little black heads with enormous eyes.

The mother grinned. 'Thanks,' she said. 'It's tough travelling without their father. But I bet they'll behave themselves now. Won't you, boys?'

The two nodded again, and Fen grinned at them. 'Good. Just be sure you do.' He turned to look for Nina, who was watching him from near the doors leading out to the street.

'What's the matter?' he asked, going up to her. 'You look as if you've just spotted the Christmas turkey eloping with the Easter ham.'

She laughed. 'No, nothing as surreal as that. I just couldn't quite believe what I was seeing. You like children, don't you?'

'Mmm. Does that surprise you?'

It did somehow. He seemed the sort of man who would be too busy taking care of business to have either the time or the patience for children. Her father had been like that. He had loved her in his way, but as a child she had always suspected he was fondest of her when she was either at school or asleep. His determination to marry her off to the first eligible man who came along was only an extension of that attitude.

'Yes, I guess it does surprise me,' Nina admitted. 'You don't seem the paternal sort somehow.'

'Oh, I don't know,' Fen drawled. 'You have to admit I'm good at keeping brats in order.' The words and his expression were bland. But when he patted her lightly on the cheek, she knew he wasn't referring to the twins.

'You,' she began, 'are the most impossibly patronizing — ' She broke off as a disembodied voice blasted over the speaker system announcing that passengers should now reboard the train.

'And are you the maternal type?' asked Fen, ignoring her interrupted outburst. He took her arm and hustled her through the jostling throng on the platform.

'I suppose I must be.' Nina felt uncomfortably warm again and almost certain that Fen knew exactly what he was doing to her blood pressure. Even his hand on her arm was enough to send it soaring. But there was no sense losing her temper. She inhaled deeply and hurried on, 'Most of my work is with disadvantaged kids. Or kids with problems.'

'Like me?' he suggested drily, dropping his hand over her hip.

'No.' Her voice came out high and breathless. 'You are neither disadvantaged nor a kid.'

'But I'm a problem?'

Yes, he was a problem, all right. And that mocking lift was back in his voice. 'You could be,' she said carefully. No doubt he would enjoy being a problem.

'I aim to please,' Fen murmured. They were outside Room A again, and before Nina could tell him she meant to go to her room to rest, he had opened the door and, putting his hand in the small of her back, had thrust her unceremoniously inside.

'Hey,' she said. 'You can't — '

'Yes, I can. You paid me to do a job. I'm the new man in your life. Remember?'

'Yes, but — '

'And in order to play the role convincingly it's high time we held a practice session.'

'Practice session?' croaked Nina. 'What kind of practice?'

'This kind.' Fen raised his arms and began to unbutton her coat.

3

Nina stood frozen beneath Fen's touch. She wanted to tell him to take his hands off her — those hands that were peeling the protective layers from her mind as briskly and efficiently as they were peeling off her coat. Her mind told her she must put a stop to his activities at once. But her mouth wouldn't open. With a strange detachment, she wondered if she was about to lose the gift she had been saving for that special man, here, in this comfortable but confining compartment.

That would be the ultimate irony. She had wanted her father to think Fen *was* that special man.

He finished with the coat and pushed it off her shoulders on to the chair. Nina gazed up at him mutely. There was an unusually bright light in his eyes, all golden and glowing and seductive. And yet gradually, as he unfastened the top button of the yellow plaid shirt she was wearing, she began to get a sense that what he had started almost as a joke, or perhaps to prove a point or to punish, had become something else. Something he had neither expected nor wanted.

Behind the golden seduction, and just before he kissed her, she saw doubt.

Then his fingers slipped under her shirt and around the back of her neck, stroking and teasing, provoking sensations only dimly dreamed before. When at last she could be silent no longer, Nina gave a low murmur of surrender, and Fen's lips closed coolly over hers.

Too coolly. There was something wrong, not as it should be — something controlled and calculating about the way he was easing his tongue into her mouth, pushing his fingers through her hair, cradling the back of her head so she couldn't move. She put her hands on his shoulders, at first in an attempt to inject warmth into an embrace that she sensed was not an embrace at all, but an experiment or — what had Fen called it? A practice.

But after only a few seconds she stopped waiting for the flare of a passion that seemed not to be there. Desire faded, and she pushed him away.

He didn't attempt to hold her, but stepped back at once. In the same moment the train swung round a corner and flung him against the window.

'Are you all right?' asked Nina, as he steadied himself.

A corner of his mouth slanted up. 'In what way?'

'I meant are you hurt.'

'Not noticeably.'

All right, if he wanted to play it that way, who was she to stop him? 'Why did you kiss me?' she asked, picking up her coat and folding it over her knee as she sat down.

Fen sank on to the sofa and immediately the room seemed larger.

He shrugged. 'Sorry. Isn't that what you paid me to do?'

Nina decided not to rise to what she suspected was an attempt to pay her back for having hired him. He might want her money, but she had a distinct feeling he thought less of her for paying it. Not that what he thought of her should matter.

It did, though.

'No,' she said. 'I paid you to spend Christmas with my family and, if necessary, to run interference when my father's latest offering becomes persistent.'

'OK. No kisses unless desperate measures are needed.' He tipped his head back and Nina noticed a thin film of sweat where his neck met the open collar of his clean cream silk shirt. 'So tell me,' he said after a brief silence, 'what do I need to know about you in order to play my part with appropriate conviction? Apart, of course, from the fact that you're used to getting your own way, and that lemon is your flavour of the season.'

'I'm not, and it isn't,' snapped Nina. She eyed him balefully, in a way wanting to forget the whole deal. That kiss had shaken her more than she was willing to admit. Because she couldn't afford to be even remotely attracted to Fen. That was the whole point in hiring him. But if she backed out now he would think he'd made her lose her nerve. Which he almost had.

She waited for her temper to cool then took a deep breath. 'All right,' she said. 'I suppose you should know that I've never had a serious romance, that I work in Seattle because it's a good long way from Chicago — I share an apartment with a friend — and that I love my job. At our house those three subjects are served up every Christmas along with the turkey and Brussels sprouts and plum pudding.'

Fen smiled. This time it was a nice smile, almost as if he actually sympathized. But he spoiled it at once by saying, 'No serious romance? That I can accept, given the general unpalatability of lemons. I can also understand that your father's objections to his daughter's dirtying her hands in a job he considers unladylike might drive you to practise your trade away from home. But why social work, for Pete's sake? What do you know about ordinary people's needs?'

Nina tried not to flinch. She didn't think Fen had actually meant to hurt her. He was just incapable of understanding that one didn't necessarily have to have experienced hunger and deprivation to know that they were bad and to want to do something about them. In a way, she supposed it was just *because* she'd had a privileged childhood that when she grew up she had wanted to give something back. But Fen's childhood had been so different that he couldn't see it. Couldn't see that she had never believed having money in the bank absolved anyone from caring about others.

But there was no point trying to explain, and in the end she said simply,

'I love children. I wanted to help.'

'Hmm.' He stared at her for a few seconds, frowning as if something puzzled him. Then he turned to gaze out of the window.

Nina studied the side of him she could see, the clearly defined bones, the droop of a heavy eyelid and the surprisingly sensitive curve of his mouth. And a sudden urge to reach out to him, to touch him on some level deeper than the merely physical, made her say quietly, 'I'm sorry your mother left you. Sorry that — well, that your life wasn't — isn't easy — '

'What?' He swung to face her, his expression a mixture of exasperation, amusement and disbelief. 'What gives you that idea?'

'You seem — bitter sometimes. And you said you work too hard — perhaps because you've never had much, and mean to have it all some day — '

'I did *not* say I work too hard. My beloved sister did. And I don't know what you mean by 'much' but whatever it is, I have plenty.'

Oh, sure. That was why he had accepted what amounted to a bribe. The only thing Fen Hardwick had much of was a misplaced pride and a stubborn refusal to acknowledge reality.

Nina's urge to give comfort evaporated.

'I'm glad to hear it,' she said.

'Mmm.' Fen eyed her sardonically. 'You know, if you look at me like that in front of your father, he'll have me thrown out of the house. And before you know it you'll be married off to the opposition.'

Nina sighed. He was right. Not about her being married off to anyone, but about the need to present an amicable and united front to her father. And if only Fen would co-operate instead of going out of his way to antagonize her, there would be no problem.

She forced herself to smile. 'He'd have trouble throwing you out, I should think. But if we can just manage to behave as though we like each other — '

'Right,' Fen interrupted. 'So start liking.' He patted his knee in invitation.

'I don't mean that way,' said Nina, exasperated. Yet she found herself biting back a smile. She thought for a moment. 'Tell me what I ought to know about *you* to make our story sound convincing.'

'Well,' he drawled, 'you could say you found me in a gutter, picked me up and dusted me off — '

'He might believe that, but he wouldn't like it,' said Nina drily. 'I mean tell me about your job, what it is you actually do. What kind of house you live in. That's the kind of thing Dad's bound to ask. Not your favourite colour or how you like your eggs.'

'Ah.' Fen stretched his arms above his head. 'My job involves buying and distributing food, travel, meetings, some personnel work and — oh, various things that come up. As to my living arrangements, I have recently sold our house and will soon be moving into an apartment. Closer to the office now that Christine doesn't need me any longer.'

'What kind of food?' asked Nina. Getting information out of Fen was like trying to open a tightly sealed jar.

'Oh, caviar, snails and chocolate bees. Some interesting sauces. Pâtés. Cheeses. That sort of thing.'

'Oh,' said Nina. 'Gourmet stuff.'

His eyes narrowed. 'You don't approve?'

She shook her head. 'I'm surprised *you* do.'

'Given my plebeian origins?' he asked, with a familiar edge to his voice.

'No, given your macho-man attitudes,' said Nina.

'I see. As it happens, a lifetime of Christine's economy casseroles gave me a taste for more exotic fare. That's the reason I chose my current line of business.'

Nina recognized a rebuke when she heard one. Once again Fen was calling her attention to the differences in their backgrounds.

'How touching. Rags to riches,' she taunted, because somehow his mild reproof had touched her on the raw.

'Watch it. Your lemon juice is leaking, Miss Petrov. It's my understanding we're supposed to like each other.' If she read the look in his eye correctly, he was about as fond of her as she was of cockroaches.

'Yes,' she agreed, looking him directly in the eye. 'But you don't like me, do you?'

She expected him to shrug and pass it off. Instead he met her look with one equally direct and said, 'I'm damned if I know. There have certainly been moments when I've been tempted to tip you discreetly off the train.' He stroked his chin, and a pensive smile began to lighten his features. 'There is one thing I'm certain of, though.'

'What's that?'

'That I'd like to take you to bed. Provided, of course, that you make it worth my while.'

'What?' Nina gaped at him, stunned and angry. But just as she was about to tell him in minute and uncomplimentary detail exactly what she thought of men who could be bought, especially for *that*, she saw his smile broaden into a grin. A taunting, attractive, maddeningly complacent grin.

As usual, Fen was baiting her. And she had swallowed the bait whole.

'What would you do if I took you up on that?' she asked, stifling an urgent desire to kick him, hard, on the nice stretch of shin that was well within range of her solid brown travelling shoe.

The grin turned into a villainous leer. 'Why don't you try it and find out,' he suggested, flexing a muscular forearm.

Nina shook her head and stood up. 'You're impossible,' she said, crossly. He'd really had her going there. And it *was* impossible to tell when he was serious and when he was merely leading her on. She still had that odd feeling that although he had allowed her to buy him, he hadn't liked it one bit.

There was something about Fenton Hardwick that didn't add up. She had felt that right from the beginning.

Hardwick . . . As she made her way over to the door, something, some nebulous memory, stirred and began to tease the back of her brain.

'What company did you say you worked for?' she asked. The train was now winding its way along the bright, crystalline shores of a nameless Upper Mississippi lake, and at that moment it gave another gentle lurch.

'I didn't. It's called F and C Foods.' Fen's gaze rested on her with unexpected intensity.

'Yes,' said Nina, frowning as she braced herself against the door-frame. 'I've heard of them, I think.'

She had, too. There was a connection somewhere, but her mind just wouldn't quite make it.

'I expect you have,' he said non-committally. His supple body seemed to relax.

'I'm off.' Nina spoke quickly, before the seductive lure of his sudden smile could weave its magic. 'I want to catch some sleep before we hit Chicago.'

'Then I'll see you later,' Fen said softly.

Nina stumbled to her room and closed the door.

There wasn't the remotest likelihood of sleep. She was too tense and restless to close her eyes. But she had needed desperately to get away from Fen. The more time she spent in his company, the more convinced she became that she had bitten off more than she could chew. And what a tasty mouthful he might have been if — if he hadn't been for sale like all the rest.

Nina sighed, and stared out at the white, frozen waters of the lake. Was it possible to become emotionally involved with a man in just two days? She had chosen him as her decoy precisely because it *wasn't* possible. And yet now she found herself unable to think of anything or anybody else. He had filled her mind almost from the moment she'd set eyes on him striding arrogantly down the platform in Seattle. But she wouldn't, *couldn't* allow herself to care for a man who could be bought. Even if he did have the face and form of an Olympian god and could melt her bones with the force of his smile.

She lifted her chin and fixed her gaze on the pearl-grey sky that hinted strongly of more snow. Then, after a few minutes of watching the passing clouds, she reached for the first of the three books she had brought to read. The books she hadn't even looked at because of Fen.

It was called *Risk Not the Heart*.

'I won't,' said Nina out loud. 'No danger of that.'

But when she went along to the lounge car shortly before lunch and saw Fen's glossy brown head bent over a curly blonde one, it hit her like a blow between the ribs that the danger wasn't as remote as she had thought.

Her first reaction was surprise, followed almost at once by a quick rush of indignation. Then, when she felt her heart beating extra fast and the blood rushing up to her ears, the truth came to her in a crushing revelation. She had not only risked her heart — she was well on her way to losing it altogether.

Nina pressed her lips together and curled her fingers into her palms. This was ridiculous. Fen was only *talking* to the girl. And the fact that he was smiling that white, irresistible smile was none of her business. Nor was it her business that the corners of his eyes were crinkled attractively with amusement.

The girl was very young. Pretty, with a pert little face that was laughing up at Fen with an admiration she wasn't attempting to disguise.

When Nina's throat muscles began to contract, she swallowed hard and made to turn away.

Fen chose that moment to look up, and as soon as he saw her he lifted a finger and beckoned.

Nina hesitated. She didn't want to talk to Fen now, wasn't sure she would be able to hide her quite inexcusable jealousy. Because that's what it was.

Jealousy. Of a girl who was flirting with a man she didn't want. Couldn't possibly want because he was precisely the sort of man she'd been avoiding for years.

Except — except that Fen *wasn't* like her father's eager suitors. On the surface he was. But . . .

No. No, there couldn't be any buts. Her problem was just a belated attack of lust. She was overdue for one, surely — had never really had one before. At least not like this. And lust she could easily deal with by heading it off at the pass.

There would have to be a slight change of plan.

When Fen beckoned again she stepped forward.

'Hi,' he said. 'Lucy, this is Nina. My fiancée. Nina, this is Lucy. We've been discussing the food in the dining-car. It's remarkably good when you consider the constraints of time and space. Don't you agree?'

Nina didn't care about the food. 'I

am not your fiancée,' she said in a cold, clear voice that caused Lucy's eyes to widen in surprise — closely followed by hopeful speculation.

'Fiancée-in-waiting then,' Fen amended, extending an arm along the back of Lucy's chair.

'You needn't bother waiting for anything,' Nina said rudely. 'Fen, I need to talk to you.'

'Talk away.' He leaned back, resting an ankle on his knee.

'Privately.'

Fen arched an eyebrow. 'I'm not sure if I should find that promising or ominous.' He turned to Lucy. 'Will you excuse us? Nina's feeling a little sour today. It happens sometimes with lemons.'

Nina, with great forbearance, managed to resist an immediate impulse to pull his burnished brown hair.

They left Lucy sitting with her mouth agape looking after them as if she thought the two of them had escaped from an institution which featured bars and padded walls.

'Where would you like us to talk?' asked Fen without much warmth. 'In your boudoir?'

'It's too small. We'll have to use yours.'

'We'll also have to make it short,' said Fen, looking at his watch. 'I don't know about you, but I have no intention of missing lunch.'

'I'll be brief,' said Nina grimly.

Fen glanced at her sharply, but said nothing. When they reached his room he held open the door with exaggerated courtesy and waited for her to precede him inside. 'Well?' he said, sliding it closed behind him. 'What is it that couldn't wait till Chicago?'

'You're not going to Chicago,' said Nina.

'Oh?' Fen hooked his thumbs into his belt and leaned against the door. He didn't ask her to sit down. 'Who says I'm not?'

'I do.'

'Do you now? And what makes you

think it's up to you?'

'Don't worry, you can keep the money,' she said disdainfully. 'But I've decided I don't need your help. I'll handle Dad's latest candidate on my own.'

'Ah. A woman of independence and courage. And what brought about this gallant change of heart? Was it something I said?'

Just about everything you said, thought Nina despairingly. Not to mention the way you look at me, the way you touch me, and the way my toes curl up just watching you drape your body against that door.

But all she said was, 'No, nothing you said. I just — don't think it will work.'

'I see.' He narrowed his eyes. 'Are you afraid I won't be able to play my part?'

'No.'

'Afraid you won't?'

'No.' The truth was that she was afraid she would be able to play it much too well.

'Then what brought on this sudden attack of independence?'

'I've always been independent. It was just that this year I thought I saw a way to make Christmas bearable. I was wrong.'

'Were you? Am I so unbearable?' His voice was low and suggestive and it made her stomach lurch.

'No, of course you're not.' She steadied herself against the wall. 'I've just decided it will be better if I deal with the problem the way I've always done. On my own.' He wasn't making this easy. She might have known he wouldn't. 'I *told* you you could keep the money,' she said irritably.

Fen bent his head and, removing his thumbs from the belt, thrust his hands deep into the pockets of his fawn trousers. When he looked up, Nina read only indifference in his eyes. 'Thank you,' he said.

'Yes.' She pushed hair that wasn't there out of her eyes. 'I — um — I guess that's it, then . . . ' Her voice trailed off. Somehow she had expected him to say more, to raise further objections. Maybe, in the end, to change her mind?

No. She refused to contemplate that. Of course she didn't want to change her mind. She was suffering from an unfortunate case of lust for a totally unsuitable man, and the only way to conquer it was to nip it smartly in the bud and get Fen out of her life before her heart suffered irreversible damage. That had to be the sensible course.

But why be sensible? whispered the devil's advocate living in her head. Sensible is so unadventurous — so dull.

Fen's voice drew her back to reality. 'Mmm,' he was saying. 'I guess it is.'

'What is what?' asked Nina blankly.

'You said that was it. I was merely agreeing.'

Nina shook her head. This whole thing was getting beyond her. Was she really going out of her mind? If she was, it would have to wait until later, because what she had to do now was get past Fen, out of this room and back to the safe haven of her compartment.

But as she stepped towards him, swaying along with the train, he put a hand around her elbow and said, 'Lunch.'

'Lunch?' repeated Nina, as electricity sizzled up her arm.

'Yes. You know, food. I'd like to eat before we hit Milwaukee.'

'Chocolate bees?' she said faintly. Wasn't that the kind of food that appealed to Fen?

'I hope not. I was thinking of a sandwich.'

'You go ahead then. I'm not hungry.'

She was, come to think of it. But she didn't want to sit down to eat with Fen. She wanted to forget about him altogether and concentrate on strategies for surviving another Christmas spent dodging her father's marital machinations.

But Fen's hand was still around her elbow and he was looking at her in a very peculiar way. As if he wasn't quite sure what he wanted to do with her, but was certain he meant to do something.

'Please let me go,' she said, in a voice that was annoyingly breathless.

Fen didn't appear to have heard her. 'Why have you lost your appetite?' he demanded. 'I haven't noticed much wrong with it up until now. Rather the opposite.'

Was he calling her a glutton? Nina glared. 'I certainly haven't lost it because of you,' she replied without pausing to think.

'I didn't suggest you had. But it's an interesting possibility.'

She didn't like the teasing glitter in his eyes any more than she liked the barely controlled quiver in his voice. Frowning, she pulled her arm away. Damn it, what was it about this man that could make her want to kiss him and kick him in the same breath?

'Excuse me,' she said, tilting her nose in the air. 'Please let me pass.'

Very deliberately Fen reached behind him to slide open the door. Even more deliberately he turned sideways so that if Nina wanted to pass him it would be impossible to avoid intimate contact.

As she started to edge forward he smiled.

4

It was the smile that was Nina's undoing.

As she tried to flatten herself into a cross between a pancake and a snake, the lazy curve of Fen's lips made her catch her breath and forget where she was putting her feet. When her brown travelling shoe came in contact with his smartly polished black one, she gasped. Fen put out a hand to steady her, but she was so anxious to escape from him that, to her dismay, her legs became entangled with his. At once erotic imaginings blossomed and began to overwhelm her. Frantic now to get away, she staggered a little and crashed out into the corridor just as a willowy young man wearing miniature skulls in his ears came drifting past the door whistling a popular tune between his teeth.

Automatically Nina's outstretched arms closed around his waist, and for a moment the two of them did a frenzied little dance in time with the motion of the train. Then the young man stumbled and they fell to the floor in an ungainly tangle of flailing arms and legs.

'Nicely timed,' drawled Fen, as Nina extricated an arm and tried to push herself upright.

'Oh! It wasn't — I didn't — ' She stopped as it dawned on her that her partner on the floor was making no attempt to get up, but appeared content to stay exactly where he was. 'I'm so sorry,' she said to him firmly. 'My fault entirely. And now I think we'd better find our feet.'

The young man leered. 'I'm not into feet.' He moved his hand a fraction until it rested unobtrusively on her hip. 'I go for the bits further up.' He shifted his hand under her rear.

'How dare — ' Nina gasped as he began to move his fingers in slow, suggestive circles. Her gaze flew upward, instinctively seeking Fen's reaction. But Fen was propped against the door-frame with his arms crossed, and he looked amused, unperturbed and totally unmoved by her predicament.

All right, thought Nina. All right. I might have known you wouldn't stir yourself to help. Taking a deep breath, she jerked herself sideways until her body was up against the wall beneath the window and only one of her legs lay trapped beneath the lustful young man's thighs. Immediately he twisted towards her.

At that point Nina heard a resigned sigh issuing from somewhere above her head. An instant later two firm hands closed around her wrists.

The next moment she was dragged upward and into Fen's arms. 'Mine, I'm afraid,' said Fen to the body on the floor. 'Beat it.'

The body took one look at Fen's face, scrambled to its feet and, as advised, beat a hasty retreat down the corridor.

'You could have helped me sooner,' grumbled Nina.

'Why? It's my understanding I was fired from my job as your bodyguard. Besides, you seemed to be enjoying yourself. I certainly was.'

'Oh! You . . . ' Nina gulped, breathed deeply and choked back the furious words. Fen was right. She *had* fired him. She was also entirely capable of looking after herself. In fact she'd been doing it for years. So why in the world, in this particular crisis, had she automatically looked to Fen for help?

She shook her head in confusion and stared at a white button on his shirt. After a while she became conscious that his arm was still around her waist.

Desire stirred deep in her belly and rippled outward. Soon her skin began to feel as if it had taken on a hot, glowing life of its own.

Slowly, very slowly, Nina raised her eyes.

Fen was looking down at her with a small furrow between his brows, as if he wasn't quite sure what she was doing in his arms.

'Yes, I did fire you,' she said woodenly. 'But I wasn't enjoying myself.'

Still the glow wouldn't go away. Which just proved she had been right in the first place when she'd decided that her first priority must be to put a safe and permanent distance between herself and Fen.

The only problem was that in this position, with her body pressed against his so that she could feel every hard, enticing inch of him, it wasn't possible to fool herself that she wanted to be *any* distance from him — certainly not a safe one.

She ran her tongue along her upper lip. 'You — you can let go now,' she finally managed to say. 'He — that creep has gone away.'

'Yes.' Fen nodded and ran an exploratory palm up and down her spine until it came to rest lightly on her rear. 'So he has. And now it's my turn.'

'You don't get a turn,' gasped Nina, as his hand continued its gentle massage.

'Don't I? Want me to stop?'

No. No, she didn't want him to stop. But he must. This was a public corridor. And she couldn't allow him to carry on his activities in private, because if he did there wasn't a doubt in her mind as to what would follow.

But why, oh, why did it have to be *this* man who had stirred to life all those feelings that up until now she had only sensed obscurely as in a dream? This man who had allowed her to buy him.

'Yes,' she groaned. 'Yes. You must stop.'

With a briskness that appalled her, he removed his hand, took her by the shoulders and turned her around.

'OK,' he said, as if it made no difference. 'I'll give you a head start. You go straight to the dining-car and find yourself a table. If you're lucky, by the time I get there, you'll be safely seated with that party from Australia I see coming up from downstairs.'

Nina saw them, too. Two tall young men and their mother, all talking at once. They looked friendly and cheerful and she didn't want to sit with them in the least. She wanted to go back to her own small compartment to cry. Except that she was damned if she was crying about Fenton Hardwick.

'I don't want to eat,' she said stubbornly — and untruthfully.

'Fine. A little fasting will probably do you good. Off you go, then.'

Dismissed. Just like that. But as Nina lifted her chin and began what she hoped was a dignified stalk back to her compartment, she thought she felt a light tap on her behind. She swung round indignantly to protest, but Fen had already disappeared into his room.

She must have imagined the tap.

Back in her compartment she sank onto the seat and buried her face in her hands.

This was ridiculous. Hopeless and

ridiculous. She had known Fen precisely two days. She wasn't in love with him, didn't want to be in love with him. And once he was out of her orbit this disturbing uncertainty would pass. Which meant that all she had to do now was stay in her compartment until the train pulled into Chicago. Then Fen would make his connection with the New York train as planned, and that would be the end of an interlude that had been — just a minor mistake. Nothing more.

But when, a half hour later, Nina's stomach began to growl insistently, it occurred to her that there wasn't, and never had been, anything remotely minor about Fen. Or about her appetite, for that matter. She was hungry. Very hungry. But if she went to the dining-car now she was bound to encounter Fen tucking smugly into a sandwich. And she didn't want to see Fen again. Ever. Nor did she want to confirm for him what she suspected he already knew — that she had no more wish to bypass lunch than he had, and that it was the thought of his company that had made her take what was, for her, an unusual decision to pass up food.

In the end she decided pride and her peace of mind were both more important to her than lunch.

When the train stopped in Milwaukee, she drew the blind and willed herself to sleep. An hour or two after that, and a little late due to a fresh snowfall, the Empire Builder trundled into the terminal in Chicago.

★   ★   ★

'I might have known,' muttered Nina, as she spotted the uniformed man in the peaked cap standing beside a waiting limousine. 'Doesn't Dad ever give up?'

Of course, as she knew very well, her father never gave up, and every year they went through the same performance. She would tell Joseph she intended to take a taxi like everyone else, and he would ignore her and send a limo. He refused to hire a chauffeur because he insisted on driving himself, but somehow he never quite found the time to meet his daughter.

Ignoring the wary glances of fellow passengers as she muttered past them, she walked up to the limo driver and laid her two small suitcases at his feet. 'Nina Petrov,' she said. 'I see my father sent you as usual.'

When the driver only blinked and lifted his cap, she shrugged and climbed into the car without waiting for his help. She gave a sigh of relief as she relaxed into the soft leather of the limo's supple seat, for a moment grateful for Joseph's interference. This was a lot easier than looking for a taxi. She closed her eyes and leaned her head back — and was immediately engulfed in a wash of overwhelming desolation. If it had had anything to do with the annual battle with her father that loomed ahead, she could have born it. But she knew it hadn't.

'I hate you, Fen Hardwick,' she groaned.

At that precise moment, the door beside her swung wide, letting in a blast of winter air. 'Do you?' said a man's familiar baritone. 'That wasn't the impression I had.'

Nina's eyes flew open. Fen, once again the ultimate executive in grey, was swinging himself and a briefcase in beside her.

'Get out,' she said, sliding to the far side of the seat. 'At once.'

'Certainly not.' Fen set the briefcase carefully on the seat.

'Driver,' called Nina to the man in front who was busily warming up the engine. 'Don't leave for a moment, please. This gentleman is just getting out.'

'No, I'm not,' said Fen, folding his arms and crossing his legs in a way that told Nina he didn't plan to move. 'Keep going, driver. The Petrov residence, please.'

'Fen.' Nina spoke in a clear, precise voice so there would be no possibility of his mistaking her meaning. 'If you don't leave at once I'm going to call station security.'

'Go ahead,' he said.

'Don't you understand?' She was practically baring her teeth at him. 'I want you out of here. Now.'

'That's too bad, isn't it? Because I have no intention of getting out of my own limousine.' He leaned back, crossed an ankle over his knee and shut his eyes.

Nina gaped at him. 'It can't be your limo,' she protested. 'Dad sent it. He always does.'

'Yes, but when I enquired I discovered your father and I use the same limo service. I called from Milwaukee and cancelled yours. I assure you this *is* my car.'

He still had his eyes closed. Nina contemplated hitting him over the head with his own briefcase and climbing out. But they were already attracting surreptitious attention from passers-by, and this holiday season promised to be difficult enough already without the appearance in the papers of snide little articles about the love life of Joseph Petrov's daughter. The fact that she had no love life to speak of wouldn't cut the slightest bit of ice with any gossip columnist worth his or her salt. And the car was already pulling out from the curb.

'How *dare* you?' Nina was so angry she was almost spitting. 'How dare you cancel my father's car?'

Fen opened an eye and turned his head towards her. 'Easy,' he said drily. 'It was simply a matter of picking up the phone.'

His smile was so coolly complacent that Nina had to look away to prevent herself from punching him on the nose. She didn't believe in violence as a solution to personal problems, but in this case . . .

Damn him. She glared at the passing traffic, thankful that no one could see her face, which no doubt resembled that of a furious porcupine on the warpath.

Fen could think he'd won a victory if he liked. But there was no way he would be allowed through her father's door without an invitation. Which he was *not* going to get. She squared her shoulders. In the meantime, since she didn't seem to have a lot of choice, she would just have to endure his company for the duration of the drive.

She stared at the falling snow which was subtly blurring the hard angles of the skyscrapers, transforming the elevated railway that formed Chicago's central Loop into a magical bridge to the stars. And she tried to ignore the man beside her. He wasn't touching her, but she could feel his presence just as if he was. And although he wore no discernible aftershave, the scent of him seemed to fill the car.

Soon they were driving north along the familiar shoreline of Lake Michigan. And Nina began to feel a new kind of tension — one that for a change had nothing to do with Fen.

In a short while they would be at her family home on the elegant old street where so many of Chicago's rich and famous lived. And the closer they came to that home, the greater her feeling of oppression. She always felt this way at Christmas.

Only this year it was worse.

'Why did you insist on coming?' she asked Fen, breaking a silence that crackled with a tension that came entirely from her side of the car. 'I told you I didn't want your help.' It was dark outside now, and she watched the bare branches of the trees swaying gently in the glow from the streetlights.

She felt rather than saw Fen shrug. 'Maybe I needed an excuse to get off that damned train.'

'Oh.' Unaccountably, Nina's shoulders sagged. 'That doesn't make sense.'

'It makes a lot of sense. Christine will understand perfectly when she hears that I gave up my ticket to New York for the sake of an exceptionally sour but pretty lemon. In fact, she'll be delighted.'

He was laughing at her. She knew he was.

'Especially a lemon who has Joseph Petrov for a father,' she said bitterly, not even caring that he had called her pretty.

'Especially,' he agreed. Nina noted that he no longer sounded amused.

'You'd no right to cancel my car,' she said. 'Not when I'd already told you I wouldn't be needing you.'

'Is that so? But, you see, I tend to make decisions based on my own needs. And as you've just pointed out, you *are* Joseph Petrov's daughter.' He reached across to cup her chin with the fingers of one hand, and when she was forced to face him he added softly, 'Don't tell me you're indifferent to my charms.'

'What charms?' asked Nina, flinching at his touch.

'Want me to show you?' His voice was soft, silky, charged with a seductive kind of menace.

'No.' She shrank back against the door, then remembered she wasn't some timorous maiden from a Victorian novel and sat up straight, looking him squarely in the eye. 'No, I don't want you to show me anything, Fen Hardwick. I just want you to — to . . .'

'Take my money and run? Not a chance.'

'But — '

She broke off because the limo was turning into the driveway of her father's house.

Nina threw her head back and filled her lungs with air. Home. The Petrov house. No example, this, of Frank Lloyd Wright's influence on the Chicago architectural scene. Joseph's house subdued nature rather than becoming a part of it. Like Joseph himself, it was large, rectangular and solid, made of weathered brick ascending three storeys to the plain pitched roof. Its windows, too, were solid and rectangular, arranged in military rows on either side of a white-pillared door. Only the ancient evergreens rising gracefully from the manicured lawns — and at this season hung with coloured lights — lent an air of grace and permanence to her childhood home.

'Mmm,' murmured Fen. 'Respectable and definitely no-nonsense. I shall look forward to meeting your father.'

'You're not going to meet him,' said Nina. 'This is the end of the road.' She glanced at her watch. 'And now, as I'm already late, I hope you won't mind if I say good night. And goodbye.' She held out her hand, but when Fen didn't take it she dropped it at once and turned to the door which the driver was holding open.

Fen didn't wait for the driver but emerged at once from his side of the car.

'I said you're not coming in,' warned Nina. She turned towards the house, afraid to look at him again in case her resolve to be rid of him weakened.

'Just a moment.' Fen's voice was quiet but commanding. 'You've forgotten something.'

Nina stopped. She didn't want to, but she couldn't help herself. Reluctantly she swivelled around. 'I haven't . . .' she began. Then she frowned. Fen was holding out a white slip of paper. 'What's that?'

As she continued to frown in perplexity, he took her hand, turned it over and placed the piece of paper on her upturned palm. Then he closed her fingers around it and stepped back.

The whole operation was conducted in silence by the light of the stars and the twin lamps standing sentinel by the door.

Slowly Nina uncurled her fingers. And there, slightly crumpled, lay the cheque she had given Fen to play the part of this year's Christmas suitor.

'What . . . ?' She stared down at it in total bewilderment. 'I don't understand. I said you could keep it. Why are you giving it back?'

A sudden breeze blew the shadow of a tree branch across Fen's face so that all she could see was the very faint gleam from his eyes. It wasn't a gleam she trusted. But when she started to move away he took a sudden step forward and hauled her into his arms.

'This is why,' he said roughly, and covered her lips with his own.

For a moment Nina was too startled to react. She stood totally still, wrapped in the warmth of his embrace, unaware of the coldness of the night, of the limo driver watching in amazement, or of anything except the feel of his firm lips on hers and the soft wool of his cashmere coat against her cheek. But as his kiss deepened, and she felt his tongue begin a more insistent probing, she remembered where she was, and who *he* was, and that some hours ago she had dismissed him from her life.

She started to struggle. 'Don't,' she cried, tearing her mouth away. 'Don't. You have no right. I told you — '

'What you told me was a lot of lemon-flavoured drivel.' He settled her head more securely on his shoulder, tightened an arm around her waist and dropped the other one down across her hips. Now she was plastered so firmly against him that if it hadn't been for the barrier of their coats she would have been able to feel every sinuous muscle in his body. He was moulding her to him as if he truly believed that was where she belonged.

Fen wasn't a man who was easily dismissed.

After a while Nina stopped even thinking of resistance because he was kissing her so thoroughly, with such burning expertise that she no longer knew what resistance was. Or what thought was. She knew only the unbelievable ecstasy of being kissed by the one man in the world who had the power to bring every singing nerve in her body to traitorous life.

She returned his kiss with passion, if not with expertise, and when her soft, delirious moans began to drift out into the night, the limo driver, with a smile and a shake of his head, climbed back into his car and drove away.

Vaguely, Nina was aware of his departure. But only vaguely. And if Fen noticed he gave no sign. Instead he deepened his kiss and moved an arm up to tangle his gloved fingers in her hair.

He was just beginning to slide his free hand with delicious sensuality over her rear when she became conscious that the night was brighter than it had been. Then she remembered that a second ago she had heard a sound that might have been the faint creaking of a door.

Slowly, too slowly, reality returned, as she realized that Fen, without haste or apparent embarrassment, was calmly straightening her coat. When he had finished he took her hand in his and turned her to face the two figures standing frozen in shock at the top of the wide, white steps leading up to the door.

Briefly, time stood still. Then the abrasive bellow of Joseph's voice shattered the tenuous peace of the winter night.

'Nina? Nina! What the *hell* do you think you're doing?' He paused to run a gimlet-sharp gaze over Fen, who had placed a casually protective arm around Nina's shoulders. 'And who in the hell is this?' Without waiting for an answer he stormed on. 'Don't you realize you're an hour and a half late, miss? If you'd taken a plane like everyone else, you could have been here two days ago.'

As Joseph growled to a halt, the optimistic notes of 'Joy to the World' rang out pure and sweet from the throats of a small group of carollers advancing with relentless seasonal cheerfulness down the street.

Both Fen and Joseph looked as though they wished they could lay their hands on something to throw.

5

Fen's grip tightened around Nina's hand, offering support, and she was surprised to feel a quick glow of gratitude. Gratitude wasn't an emotion she was used to in connection with Fen. But he seemed to understand that she had always hated being late, and that her father's accusation rubbed her where it hurt.

She opened her mouth, meaning to point out that she had never had any intention of arriving two days earlier. But she heard herself saying instead, 'I'm sorry, Dad. The train was held up by the snow.'

'That's what I mean, girl. If you'd taken a plane — '

'I know, but — '

'Leave it to me,' murmured Fen, who didn't seem in the least put out at being caught kissing the daughter of the house in full view of any member of the household who cared to watch.

Nina looked up at him, startled, but before she could ask what he meant, she heard him saying evenly, 'Nina took the train because I asked her to travel with me, sir. I have to be in New York on the twenty-seventh, so I thought we might spend some time together first.'

Joseph's grey eyes seemed about to bulge out of his head. Seeing her domineering father for once at a loss for words, Nina had to struggle hard not to choke.

But Joseph noticed her struggle and scowled. 'What are *you* laughing about?' he demanded, recovering quickly from incipient apoplexy.

'Joy to the earth! The Saviour reigns,' chorussed the carollers.

'Now, Joseph.' Nina's small, blonde mother, Nancy, who up until this point had been quietly hanging back behind her husband, hurried to soothe ruffled family feathers. 'You know Nina always takes the train. She enjoys it.'

'Harrumph. Not the only thing she seems to enjoy.' Joseph turned his scowl on Fen. 'What do you think you're talking about, young man? I won't have my daughter taken advantage of.'

'Of course not, sir,' Fen said gravely. He touched a black-gloved hand to Nina's cheek. 'Was I taking advantage of you, Nina?'

For a moment she was speechless. Oh, yes, he'd taken advantage of her, all right. He was still doing it, and she felt as if her insides had been turned inside out and hung out to dry in a hurricane. All the same, to the best of her recollection, Fen was the only man she had ever met who wasn't intimidated by Joseph. Since he could obviously look after himself, there was no reason for her not to pay him back.

'Yes,' she said demurely. 'I'm afraid you were.'

In the background Joseph started to rumble, and Nancy made an anxious twittering noise.

'Oh?' said Fen, glancing pointedly at

the cheque that, incredibly, was still crushed in Nina's hand. 'Funny. I could have sworn it was the other way around.'

Nina moistened her lips. He wasn't joking now. 'I thought I was doing you a favour. Not taking advantage,' she said quietly.

'Is that so? By allowing me to kiss you?'

'No, I meant — '

'The cheque? Yes, I see. But I'm afraid being bought like some over-priced gigolo isn't my personal idea of a favour.' He spoke pleasantly but with an undertone of very dry ice. 'Of course I realize you've been brought up to think everyone has their price — but it happens not to be true.'

Did he mean it? Nina shook her head in bewilderment. She glanced at the cool slant of his eyebrows, noted the arrogant tilt of his head. He sounded sincere enough. But, damn it, he *had* taken the money.

She felt her normally equable temper

coming to the boil.

'If the shoe fits, wear it,' she snapped. 'You weren't hard to acquire. I've picked mushrooms that put up more resistance.'

'Nina!' Joseph's roar thundered down the steps like a concrete drill on full power. 'What the devil is going on? If you owe this fellow money, then pay him and tell him to beat it. If he owes you — I'll take care of him. But your mother and I will not stand out here in the snow while the two of you conduct negotiations in my driveway — '

Only the hard pressure of Fen's fingers on her palm told Nina that her gibe about mushrooms had hit home.

'Mr. Petrov,' he said crisply, interrupting the flow. 'The only thing Nina owes me is an apology. The only thing I owe her is some straight talking. And, like you, I would prefer to see both those debts settled at once.'

Dad's going to explode, thought Nina, watching Joseph's cheeks inflate like pink balloons. She found herself reluctantly admiring Fen's audacity. But when she saw her mother anxiously chewing her lip and twisting her hands at her waist she felt a quick stirring of conscience.

It *was* cold out here in the snow. And of course it was time to bring this absurd Christmas charade to an end. If that could only be achieved by allowing Fen to have his way — again — then so be it.

She turned to look up at her parents. 'This is Fenton Hardwick,' she said formally. 'Fen, my mother and father, Nancy and Joseph Petrov.'

Joseph's eyes narrowed, and suddenly he looked a little less explosive. His keen gaze swept over Fen. 'Hardwick?' he said. 'Hmm. All right, you'd better come in.'

'Thank you,' said Fen. 'I hope it's not an imposition.'

'When has *that* ever bothered you?' muttered Nina.

Fen responded by tapping her lightly on the rear, and Joseph at once replied

124

heartily, 'No, no. No trouble at all. We were expecting young Vickery. He was supposed to be coming for dinner. But the damn fool's got himself engaged. Says he can't make it. Told him I wouldn't have it, but . . . '

Saved by Cupid's arrow, thought Nina, resisting an unwise urge to laugh hysterically. After all the trouble I've taken to protect myself from unwanted advances, this year's suitor isn't going to come up to scratch. I needn't have enlisted Fen's services at all.

'Well, come in, come in,' urged Joseph. 'Not getting any warmer out here.'

Fen raised an eyebrow at Nina and picked up two of the suitcases the limo driver had left in the driveway. 'After you,' he said, inclining his head gravely. 'I believe lemons take precedence over mushrooms.'

Nina gaped at him, too startled to hide her stupefaction. But when she saw a small, malevolent grin part his lips, she turned her back on him so he wouldn't see her own lips curve up in response. Damn him. Did he *have* to keep making her laugh? As she marched regally up the steps, it was only the knowledge that he was likely to retaliate that prevented her from following her instincts and turning round to deliver an unladylike punch to his hard midriff.

'And makes the nations prove the glories of His righteousness and wonders of His love,' trilled the carollers as Fen and Nina reached the top step.

Once they were inside, a formidable figure in black swooped down to pick up the rest of the cases, and Nina noticed that Fen relinquished his as if it had never occurred to him that he might not be spending the night.

She swallowed, uncomfortably aware that his sardonic brown eyes were surveying her with what could only be described as complacence — as if he had just scored a coup and intended very shortly to score another. She turned away with a toss of her head.

The four of them were standing in a

big, dark hallway at one end of which a steep, gold-carpeted staircase led to a three-sided gallery above. The only visible concession to Christmas was a green vase filled with holly which stood on an antique table beneath a still life featuring dead game birds and something that looked like hundred-year-old cheese.

Nina stared glumly at the holly and wondered what she'd let herself in for. When she felt a hesitant hand on her shoulder, she jumped. Then she smelled the sweet, cloying scent of lavender and spun round to fling her arms around her mother's swan-like neck.

'There, there, dear,' said Nancy vaguely, patting Nina's back as if she were a baby needing to be burped. 'Your father and I are so happy to have you home, dear. And we're delighted you've brought your young man . . . '

'He's not my young man,' wailed Nina, crumbling in the face of her mother's gentleness. 'He's a — a . . . '

'Decoy?' suggested Fen from behind

her. 'Smoke-screen? Fraud?'

'Skunk,' said Nina through her teeth.

'Now, now, Nina,' muttered Joseph. 'No need to be rude to young Hardwick. Next thing you know, you'll be asking me to have him thrown out.' He chuckled as if he'd made an excellent joke.

Nina closed her eyes as a vision of fisticuffs in the front hallway flashed improbably into her mind — with Fen thoroughly enjoying himself in the centre of a pugilistic throng of family retainers. No, she didn't want him thrown out. She wanted him to leave of his own volition.

But as she watched her father lead him into the main drawing-room with a friendly hand on the shoulder, she saw the likelihood of that happening grow dimmer with every passing moment.

'Come along, dear. You'll want to put your things away,' said Nancy. 'Your father will take care of your Mr. Hardwick.'

Her mother sounded so pleased and

happy that Nina couldn't bring herself to repeat that Fen wasn't, and never had been, 'her' Mr. Hardwick.

When she went downstairs twenty minutes later, she discovered Joseph and Fen enjoying a drink together in front of a roaring fire. Beside them stood an enormous Christmas tree with a revolving gold angel on the top.

'Ah,' said Joseph. 'There you are, Nina. Your mother's arranged a fire in the small sitting-room. More private in there if you and Hardwick — '

'We don't need to be private, Dad,' said Nina firmly. 'I don't have a lot to say to Mr. Hardwick — '

Fen's nostrils flared briefly. 'We'll see about that,' he said, putting down his glass and standing up.

'That's the spirit,' said Joseph. 'Don't put up with any of her nonsense, lad. She'll lead you a dance if you do.'

'Yes, I've noticed that,' said Fen, with a non-committal smile. 'Come on, Nina.' He took her arm firmly and led her out into the hall.

Nina didn't even think about resisting. She couldn't. Because this was far, far worse than she'd imagined.

If she read the signs correctly — and she was almost certain she did — Joseph had taken in Fen's well-cut suit and air of assurance and come to the erroneous conclusion he was marriage material. A worthy replacement for young Vickery. And there was only one thing to be done about it. She must convince Fen once and for all that she wasn't interested. After that, surely he would leave.

'Where to?' asked Fen.

Nina gestured at a door across the hall, and Fen propelled her ahead of him into a firelit sitting-room fitted with heavy, overstuffed furniture that loomed massively in the glowing orange light.

'So you don't have much to say to me,' he said, clicking the door shut and leaning against it as if he expected her to stage a panic-stricken break-out.

'No. Not much.' She started to edge

away from him. He looked terribly grim, and she didn't trust the dark glitter of his eyes in the firelight.

'I see,' said Fen. 'Then perhaps a different kind of communication will work better.'

No, thought Nina, as he moved purposefully towards her. No. Not again.

It was her last coherent thought before Fen's arms were wrapped around her back and she lost the will to do anything but respond to the virile body entwined so intimately with hers.

The touch of Fen's lips was as drugging and overwhelming as it had been when he had kissed her in the driveway. But now that they were no longer wrapped in heavy winter coats, there was an immediacy to their contact that set the blood singing in her ears. She could feel every lean inch of him against her softness — and when his hand closed over the silk shirt covering her breasts, this time no roaring father appeared to shatter the seductive closeness of the moment.

'Fen,' murmured Nina, shifting her hips against him as his teasing fingers began to drive her wild. 'Fen . . . ' Her hunger was explicit. And yet she didn't know what it was exactly that she wanted — what she waited so eagerly to receive . . .

Then, when she was certain she wouldn't be able to bear the waiting and the incompleteness a moment longer, Fen let her go.

'There,' he said. 'That should loosen your tongue.'

It didn't at first. Nina discovered that although she could open her mouth, no sound would come out. But when the room stopped spinning, and she finally regained the power of speech, words were tumbling from her lips like water streaming over a dam.

'Yes,' she said. 'It's loosened it all right. Fen Hardwick, you are without a doubt the rudest, most indefensibly self-satisfied man I have ever known. *And* the most arrogant and bossy — '

'That,' interrupted Fen, 'is not what I'd call an apology.' He settled his shoulders more firmly against the door.

'It wasn't meant to be. Why should I apologize? I bought you, didn't I?'

'No, as a matter of fact you didn't.'

'Oh? And I suppose you expect me to believe that you came home with me just to give me back my money.'

'Why else?'

'For the sake of a bigger pay-off, of course,' She hated the break in her voice and attempted to steady it. 'Once you discovered I was a sucker for your kisses, you figured I'd be ripe for the plucking. You're not married, my father is Joseph Petrov III. And he seems to have fallen for your line. That's why you came after me, isn't it?'

A log cracked in the fireplace, and Nina took in for the first time that they were glowering at each other in semi-darkness.

It didn't matter.

Fen reached behind him, flicked a switch and flooded the room with revealing light. Nina screwed up her eyes against the glare.

'Would you like to say that again?' he asked quietly.

'No,' said Nina, warily studying the harsh lines etched into his face. 'I wouldn't. I've said all that needs to be said. Let me pass, please.'

'Why? So you can run to your most estimable father and spill the beans? He won't believe you, you know.'

'He might,' said Nina, feeling drained and cold in spite of the warmth of the fire. 'You won't be the first fortune-hunter he's sent packing.'

'Thank you.' Fen gave her a small, sarcastic bow. 'I've never been called a fortune-hunter before.'

'Then I've enlarged the scope of your experience,' said Nina with deceptive sweetness. 'Now, are you going to let me pass, or do I have to scream?'

He shrugged. 'Want something to scream about? It'll make it much more convincing.'

'What I want,' said Nina, ignoring the

bright challenge in his eyes, 'is for you to move.'

'Sure?'

'Of course I'm sure.'

Fen's mouth flattened, but he stepped back and swung open the door. As Nina scurried past him she heard him murmur, 'Get rid of the blinkers, Nina, and face the truth.'

She stopped dead. 'What's that supposed to mean?'

'It means that instead of walking tall, and accepting that there are plenty of men who might just want you for yourself — for your compassion and your independence and your strength — you've chosen to wear your mistrust like a badge of honour and assume the worst of every man who comes along. And one of these days you'll find no one comes any more. Your father understands that. Even if you don't.'

Nina lifted her chin a little higher and didn't answer. The last thing she wanted to hear at this moment was that, inexplicably, her father and Fen had become allies. That her wonderful scheme had so hopelessly backfired.

She didn't look back to see if Fen was watching, but hurried up to her room at the head of the stairs. *Had* her scheme backfired? Had her father really been taken in by Fen?

'It doesn't make *sense*,' she groaned out loud. 'Dad's no fool. He *must* see that Fen isn't one of his executive hot shots. He must, because if he doesn't . . . Oh, my God!' She sank down on her blue quilted bedspread and put both hands up to her face.

Was it possible that *Joseph* had planted Fen on the train? Was young Vickery nothing more than a — a red herring? Had her father, all along, been playing a game with her? Could he be that devious?

Could Fen be? Her lips tightened and she bunched her hands into fists and pounded them into the pillow. Oh, she wouldn't put it past either of those two. Not for a moment. And *that* would explain why Fen had been so determined to hand her money back.

To her horror, Nina felt tears pricking at her eyes. They were partly tears of rage, but mixed with the rage was a terrible feeling of desolation and betrayal. Because if Fen was really Joseph's man, that meant he was just another ambitious suitor on the make. And in spite of all her efforts to pretend otherwise, in her heart she had never wanted that to be true.

A clock chimed loudly in the hall, and Nina jumped and glanced at her watch.

Dinner time. It was always served promptly in Joseph's house, and if she didn't move fast she'd be late. As for Fen . . . No, she didn't want to think about Fen.

She showered hastily — no time for a leisurely bath — and pulled on a soft, cream wool dress with long sleeves. Then she attached the ruby pendant and earrings she didn't often have a chance to wear and hurried downstairs to the drawing-room.

Fen, Joseph and Nancy were finishing pre-dinner drinks. 'Just in time,' said Joseph, not offering a drink to his daughter. 'Shall we go in?' He took Nancy's arm and the four of them moved sedately down the hall to the dining-room.

Fen made no attempt to take Nina's arm. 'You're looking very glamorous,' he remarked as they sat down. 'Not for my benefit, I assume?'

'You assume right,' snapped Nina.

Fen's eyes gleamed, and she knew that once again she'd fallen into a trap.

Dinner was a scrupulously polite affair that sizzled with tension beneath the civilized veneer of discussion about the journey and the weather. Nina noticed that her father kept throwing speculative glances at Fen, and that Nancy kept giving him nervous smiles. Were they wondering if Fen had succeeded where others had failed? Were they trying to decide if he would do for their daughter? Or had Joseph decided that long ago?

For his part, Fen appeared oblivious to the unspoken currents circling all around him, and joined in the conversation with an easy charm that made Nina want to hit him.

She spoke very little herself, and as soon as dinner was over, Joseph announced that he and his wife were planning an early night. 'Leave you young people to yourselves,' he said, beaming as if he were Santa Claus handing out presents.

'Dad, you never go to bed before ten,' protested Nina.

'Your mother is — um — tired,' said Joseph, looking shifty. 'Hardwick, I suggest you use the small sitting-room again. We've kept the fire going.'

Before Nina could offer further objections, Joseph had taken Nancy by the hand and towed her out into the hall.

'All right. Your move,' said Nina once they were alone. She couldn't quite keep the bitterness from her voice.

Fen was leaning against the wall with his hands plunged deep into the pockets of his elegant grey trousers. His mouth looked as though it had been drawn by a ruler. But after a few seconds he jerked his head peremptorily at the hallway, and Nina decided there was nothing to be gained by refusing to talk.

As soon as they were back in the small room with the fire, she edged away from him and sank into a red brocade chair by the hearth. Then after a while she heard his footsteps on the carpet and sensed that he had come up behind her.

'What do you want from me, Fen?' she asked tiredly. When he didn't answer she tilted her head back. He was bending over her, and she could feel his warm breath on her cheek.

'I'm not sure I want anything,' he said. Nina stiffened, and almost absently he dropped a hand over the soft swell of her breast, as he added thoughtfully, 'Although I did, at one point, think I might want you in my bed. Possibly on a permanent basis.'

'Permanent? I'm flattered,' said Nina, automatically tensing beneath his touch. 'Particularly as you've only known me for a few days. But I do, of course, see the obvious benefits of being married to Joseph Petrov's daughter.'

The hand stroking her breast clenched convulsively and was immediately withdrawn. 'Yes,' Fen agreed, so coldly that she flinched. 'So you've already said. And I'm afraid I haven't the patience to wait for you to discover your mistake.'

Nina twisted around, trying to see his face, but he had stepped back into the shadows. 'What mistake? Did my father set this up?' she asked wearily. 'Did he arrange for you to be on the train?'

Fen was so long answering that for a while Nina thought he'd left the room. Then his voice seemed to come to her from a distance. 'No, Nina, he didn't. We've never met before. And to save you the trouble of asking, he also knows

I'm not remotely interested in your money.'

There was a bleakness in the way he spoke, a cold withdrawal, that stirred an answering coldness in her heart. And suddenly she *knew*. With chilling clarity. Fen was telling her the truth. Had probably been telling it all along. She wasn't sure why she knew now, when she hadn't believed him before. It had come as a kind of revelation.

She reached for him blindly, then realized he was still speaking.

'There's something else you should know before I leave.'

'What's that?' Nina whispered. Fen was leaving? When there was so much still left unsaid? She wanted to tell him . . . She shook her head, trying to remember what it was she had to say.

'You should understand,' Fen was explaining, 'that when I accepted your commission on the train, it was as the joke you didn't see it was. And partly, I admit, to pay you back. It's not flattering to be mistaken for Rent-a-Stud of the Week. I thought you could do with the lesson.'

Very slowly Nina lifted her head and turned to face him. He was standing with his hand on the doorknob. His mouth was curved in a smile, but his eyes were as blank as one-way glass.

'I *don't* understand,' she said at last, tracing her finger round a red brocade leaf.

'No. I see that.' Fen shut his eyes. 'Perhaps I expected too much.'

'What *did* you expect?' Nina was too lost and confused to think straight any more.

His mouth turned down. 'That you would realize I'd never have kept your money — even if I'd needed it. Which, as it happens, I don't.' He paused, then seemed to make up his mind. 'Remember F and C Foods?'

Nina nodded. 'Yes. You work for them.' She frowned. Wasn't there something else? Something she'd tried to remember? Something about — oh, yes, now she had it. The company had donated an extraordinarily generous supply of foodstuffs for the agency's Christmas hampers for needy families. She had supplied some of the names of the recipients herself. And the food hadn't been useless things like caviar and chocolate-covered bugs. She remembered all the staff had been delighted at how practical and yet imaginative F and C's selections had been.

F and C . . . F, the president, had made the delivery himself, according to a starry-eyed receptionist who had waxed poetic about muscled shoulders heaving boxes, and a delectable masculine backside displayed to great advantage as the boxes were shifted into place. The receptionist had also gushed breathlessly about glossy brown hair and eyes like an evening in autumn . . .

Oh, God! F! Fenton. F and C. Fenton and Christine? Could it be . . .

She raised her eyes to Fen's coldly blank face.

And had her answer.

'You *are* F and C Foods. Aren't you?' she groaned with despairing certainty. 'You don't just work for them.'

'No,' said Fen. 'I don't. At least not in the way you mean — and not that there's anything wrong with honest work.'

'Of course there isn't. Because you're the president. It's your company. Your very *successful* company. You *didn't* need my money. *That's* why you gave it back. Not because you wanted to marry Joseph Petrov's daughter.'

'Go to the top of the class.'

Fen stared down at her impassively, and when he didn't seem inclined to continue, she demanded with a kind of desperation, 'Why didn't you tell me before? I can understand why you couldn't resist taking me up on my offer. It must have seemed a joke to you at first. And like you said, a way of teaching me how foolish it is to make superficial judgements. But later — '

'Later you were too busy playing Lady Nose-in-the-Air dismissing the upstart servant. I saw no reason to waste my time on explanations you obviously weren't willing to listen to. Besides . . . ' he smoothed a hand over his jaw. 'It seemed a shame to waste such a virtuoso performance.'

Nina ignored the taunt. 'But you still cancelled my father's limousine,' she said, twisting the pendant at her neck.

'Mmm. I had this misguided idea that in spite of your background and general perversity, maybe I'd at last found a woman I might make time for. Once she'd got over the idea I was for sale.' He shrugged. 'Apparently I was wrong.'

Nina hadn't thought brown eyes could look so passionless, or that Fen's seductive body could seem so unapproachable.

Had her suspicions and accusations gone too far? Fen, with his quirky sense of humour and his contempt for the rich and the spoiled, had been playing a game with her all along. Oh, he hadn't intended to be cruel, that wasn't his

146

way. But how could he possibly have understood what it was like to grow up in Joseph Petrov's shadow, to have spent most of your young adulthood fighting tooth and nail for every inch of independence you gained? And how could he have understood about the suitors?

Fen, after all, was a man.

A man who was already halfway through the door and about to walk out of her life.

She stood up, but the door was already closing in her face.

Nina stared at it, heard it snap shut — felt her heart slump down to her red shoes. And that was when she knew for sure that she didn't want Fen out of her life. It was too soon to be sure, of course. Yet she was.

Fen was the one.

And if she didn't move fast she would lose him.

The thought prodded her into action, and she skidded across the thick Turkish carpet as if a hundred crazed camels were in pursuit.

But by the time she gained the hallway, Fen had disappeared.

She glanced around, searching for a clue to his whereabouts — and heard her father's unmistakable voice saying loudly, 'Nonsense, my boy. All Nina needs is a firm hand — '

Another, quieter voice interrupted, and the rest of Joseph's speech was cut off.

Nina gazed, mesmerized, at the closed door of the drawing-room. Fen must have told Joseph he didn't mean to marry his daughter. And Joseph was trying to persuade him otherwise, telling Fen how to handle her. As for Fen's hands, firm or otherwise . . .

His voice, brisk and businesslike, interrupted her wayward imaginings. 'I agree, sir. Nina could certainly do with — '

'A good boot in the right place,' said her father. 'I have faith in you, Hardwick. You can manage her.'

'It's a tempting thought,' Nina heard

Fen admit. 'Although that wasn't exactly what I had in mind. And as I'm not given to violence, I'm afraid . . . '

She didn't hear any more, because a lump, hard and painful, was beginning to form in her throat. Dammit, how *could* those two arrogant men — and particularly Fen — stand there discussing her as if she were a horse? A horse that he was obviously unwilling to train. It was evident from the dry politeness of his voice. And if he thought . . .

All at once the lump in her throat burst. And a rage that was part agonizing grief because she knew she'd lost him, and part resentment that both Fen and her father seemed to think she was a commodity to be *managed*, rose up to propel her through the drawing-room door. She'd show Fen. He might not want her, but by the time she was through with him, one way or another, she would have him grovelling in the dust at her feet.

She didn't pause to reflect that grovelling and Fen didn't go together.

Nor was dust permitted to settle in Joseph's house.

In the end it didn't matter, because when she came to a stop on the threshold, she saw at once that Fen was already at her feet — although not in supplication or surrender. He was searching for something among the array of colourful packages piled beneath the huge Christmas tree.

Briefly, very briefly, Nina was reminded of the receptionist's comment about a delectable male backside bending over boxes. After that, all she could think of was her overpowering need to let Fen know exactly what she thought of him. Not that she knew what she thought of him any longer. She just knew his dismissive comments hurt. Unbearably.

'Skunk,' she said, very clearly and precisely. 'Fenton Hardwick, did anyone ever tell you you're a skunk?'

Fen, looking hard and formidable in his grey executive suit, rose smoothly and deliberately to his feet.

Nina swallowed and squeezed her

eyes shut. He wasn't a skunk. He was a strong, beautiful man. And all she wanted to do was throw her arms around him.

'Here it is, Mrs. Petrov.' Fen ignored Nina and handed a topaz brooch to Nancy with a smile. 'The clasp must have come loose while you were decorating.'

'Oh, thank you so much. My eyes aren't what they used to be, you see.'

Nina glanced sideways to where Joseph was standing beside a solid Victorian table with a lot of carved scrollwork around the edge. His gaze flicked keenly from Fen to his daughter.

'Ah, there you are, my dear,' he said blandly. 'Your mother and I were just off to bed.'

'You've already used that one,' said Nina.

'Have I? Well, well.' He smiled innocently. 'Good night, my dear. Good night, Hardwick. I'm glad you made things clear to our little girl. Come along, Nancy.'

'Wait a moment.' Nina swallowed. 'What — what was that you said? About making things clear?'

Joseph cleared his throat. 'Humph. Young Hardwick here. Knew who he was the moment you introduced him. Heard about his career. Started as a stock-boy, worked his way up to the top, then bought the company. I admire that kind of ambition.' He scratched his head and tried to look artless. 'Could see you'd no idea, though.'

'Dad! Then why didn't you *tell* me?'

Joseph cleared his throat again. 'Didn't think you'd like it. Haven't liked it when I've approved of other young fellows.'

'But they were different. They — ' Nina stopped abruptly, because Joseph's smug smile was practically splitting his face.

'That's what I thought,' he said, nodding. 'Different.' Then, seeing Nina's furious expression, he said, 'Nancy. Let's go.'

'Now, Joseph.' Nancy threw an

anxious glance at her daughter. 'I don't think Nina wants — '

'Yes, she does,' said Joseph. 'Take my word for it.'

'Well . . . '

But Joseph already had his wife by the hand, and as she was no match for his determination to remove her from the scene, a minute later Nina was once again alone in a firelit room with Fen. Only this time the fireplace was bigger and made of stone, and Fen was gripping the back of a wing chair looking as if he was about to deliver a stern lecture on manners, deportment and the respect due to presidents of companies that imported fine food.

Nina put her hands behind her back. The indignation she had felt on hearing Fen discuss her with her father was still there. But it wasn't *entirely* Fen's fault — and somehow it didn't seem to matter much any more. Only one thing mattered. Perhaps, in her heart, she had known that all along.

'*You* forgot something this time,' she

said quietly. If she didn't get to the point at once she would lose her nerve. And Fen might actually get round to that lecture.

'Did I?' he asked. 'I doubt it. Your mother said she'd see my suitcase was brought down. All I have left to do is call a taxi.'

Nina shook her head. 'No, that's not what I meant. There's something else.'

Fen glanced at his watch. 'Then you'd better tell me. I've a flight to catch.' His goldstone eyes were about as promising as a cobra's.

Nina took a deep breath and lifted her chin to give herself courage. 'You forgot the apology you said I owed you.'

Only a brief twitch of his eyebrows betrayed that he was taken by surprise. 'So I did,' he agreed. 'I suppose it seemed a little meaningless in the circumstances.'

'No,' said Nina. 'It isn't meaningless. It matters to me. I should have known when you gave back my — my bribe

— that I'd misunderstood everything from the start.'

Fen didn't respond, just looked through her as though he didn't really see her. Nina had to struggle not to drop her eyes. 'I'm sorry,' she said, meaning it, but suspecting she sounded surly and defensive. 'You were quite right when you told me I've become so blinkered and mistrustful that I can't tell the pearls from the swine — '

'That's not quite the way I put it,' murmured Fen. His eyes came back into focus and he brushed a hand across his mouth.

'Well, no,' agreed Nina. Had she really seen the ghost of a smile on his lips? 'I wouldn't exactly call you a pearl — '

'You called me a skunk, as I remember.'

'Yes, but never a swine. Fen, I didn't *know*. There's never been anyone — I mean, every man I've ever met who's known about my father has had his eye on a prize that isn't me. I didn't understand . . . that is . . . ' She gulped hard, trying to dislodge the lump that had come back into her throat. 'I suppose I should have seen that you weren't like all the others. I *did* see that you enjoyed teasing and provoking me and I — well, in a way I liked it — ' She broke off because Fen wasn't responding and she couldn't think of any more to say.

She couldn't blame him for not understanding. Even when he had handed her money back she had refused to see what had always been right under her nose — that although Fen had a wicked sense of humour, he was a man of integrity and compassion and pride. No wonder he'd been insulted by her bribe.

She gave a small sigh and allowed her eyes to drop. On the other side of the room, a fresh log flared in the grate, and for a moment there was an acrid smell of smoke.

Fen didn't move, and without looking up Nina murmured, 'I'll call a taxi for you,' before she turned away.

She had almost reached the door when she felt Fen's peremptory hand close on her shoulder.

'And where do you think you're going?' he asked.

'I told you — '

'Yes, and you're not doing anything of the sort.'

'But I — ' She gasped as he turned her around and placed a hand on the small of her back. 'I . . . ' She looked into his eyes, all narrowed and golden, and couldn't remember what she'd meant to say.

The muscles in her stomach began to clench, and when the room swam out of focus, automatically her body swayed towards him. Fen placed two steadying hands on her shoulders.

'Hold it,' he said, his voice coming to her softly from a distance. 'No fainting. Your father would have my scalp.'

'I never faint,' said Nina. She opened her eyes extra wide and made herself meet his gently sceptical gaze. 'And you never part with your scalp. Do you?'

'No,' he admitted. 'But I doubt that would stop your redoubtable father from giving me a run for my money. I like him, Nina.'

He stepped back and looked her over so thoroughly that after a while she felt obliged to inform him that she wasn't one of his exotic foods being considered as an addition to his stock. 'I've no intention of being added to your inventory,' she told him, a little breathlessly.

Fen ran his thumb across her lips. 'You needn't worry. Lemons are too commonplace for my shelves.'

'Oh.' Nina knew she ought to come up with a suitably deflating rejoinder. But she couldn't think of one. His teasing remark had cut too close to the bone.

'On the other hand,' said Fen, 'as I think I told you before, I do like a little tartness in my life. It keeps me from getting bored.'

His hand was on her back again, and

suddenly he moved it lower, making her gasp. Lord, she couldn't stand this much longer. She knew Fen teased out of habit, but it wasn't his teasing her body craved now. And on top of that she longed for reassurance, for some sign that he cared enough to find out if she was really a woman he might — what had he said? A woman he might finally find time for.

'I'm not here to spice up your jaded palate,' she told him, wishing he would stop whatever it was he was doing with his fingers. It was so distracting she couldn't keep her mind on the subject at hand. Which was — which was what? Dear heaven, she couldn't even think straight.

With a groan of frustration she attempted to pull out of his arms.

But Fen wouldn't let her. Instead his hand spread out across her lower back and he drew her so firmly against him that she couldn't fail to be aware of his arousal. His other hand was curved round her neck, and once again she felt as if the floor had dissolved underneath her so that Fen was her only anchor to a world that no longer had any meaning beyond his touch.

Her heart sounded loud in her ears. She could feel the blood pounding in her veins, and his invading lips were warm and wonderful and gentle — the lips of the man she wanted to spend her life with.

No. No, wait. That couldn't be true.

Now Fen was dropping feather-light kisses on her neck and along her jaw. But Nina discovered she had somehow come back to earth.

The smoky smell was stronger now. She would have to see to that fire.

'Fen,' she whispered. 'Fen, please, we can't — '

'We can,' said Fen, touching a pulse at the base of her throat. 'Maybe not here, in your parents' house. But very soon — '

'No. I don't want . . . ' Nina swallowed, unable to finish.

'What don't you want?' He smiled,

an achingly sensuous smile that tugged at her heart.

'I don't want to be just another of your handy bodies — '

Fen gave a snort of disbelief. 'Not much danger of that,' he said drily. 'So far you've been exceedingly unhandy.'

Nina tried to smile to show it didn't matter, but when the corners of her mouth began to quiver, she gave up.

At once Fen wrapped both arms around her and drew her head against his chest. 'Hey,' he said, absently stroking her hair. 'There's no need to cry, little lemon.'

'I'm not crying.' Nina sniffed loudly into his elegant grey jacket. 'And I'm not a lemon.'

'And no sniffing. Nina, look at me.' He put a finger under her chin and tilted it upwards.

Nina sniffed again, but only because he smelled so nice.

'Nina — lemon, I'm sorry, too,' he said softly.

Nina blinked. Surely the light in his

eyes was unusually bright. And his mouth — his mouth was all tender and wry.

'What are you sorry for?' she asked blankly.

'For not understanding. I couldn't see — was too blinded by my own prejudices to see — that your whole experience has been so different from mine that you were bound to be mistrustful of me at first — bound to think I was just another man on the make.' He held her away, smoothed her hair from her face and shook his head. 'Especially when I was fool enough to accept payment for services not rendered. I didn't think about your feelings much, I'm afraid. Didn't think you had any to speak of.' He gave her a rueful, self-deprecating grin.

'Thanks,' said Nina. Was she going crazy, or was this really Fen apologizing and looking at her as if she were an ice-cream he longed to melt slowly and deliciously on his tongue? She tried a smile and was vaguely surprised to find that this time it stayed on her face. 'If you had known — would it have stopped you?'

'I don't know.' His answering smile was guarded now, hinting at regret. 'Probably not. At the time I thought you could do with a good shaking up. But I found myself being shaken up instead.'

Did he mean it? Or was he only teasing again? 'What changed your mind about me?' she asked, still suspicious.

'You did,' he said promptly. 'You called me a skunk — twice — which as a term of endearment leaves something to be desired. But then you apologized so bravely and looked so sad that it came to me you must feel strongly about skunks.' He slid a finger slowly and deliberately down her spine. 'Even, perhaps, to the point of learning to trust one.'

'I do trust you,' said Nina, burying her face in his neck. She wrinkled her nose appreciatively. 'Mmm. And I had no business calling you a skunk.'

Fen twisted a lock of her hair around his hand and drew her head back. 'No, you hadn't,' he agreed. 'And I think it's time you lemons started showing a little more respect towards us skunks. You can start by kissing one.'

Nina shook her head. 'Won't do any good,' she said sweetly. 'Only frogs are supposed to turn into princes.'

'Kiss me anyway,' ordered Fen, with a gleam in his eye that promised delightful trouble if she didn't do as she was told.

Nina kissed him. And it turned out he was right, because the moment her lips touched his, she knew he would always be prince enough for her.

★　★　★

When Nina hurried into the drawing-room early on Christmas morning, she found Fen waiting for her. He was standing beneath the tree looking sexy and strokable in a soft brown sweater.

164

As soon as he saw her he held out his arms.

'Are you my Christmas present?' she asked, walking into them.

His answer was a deep and passionate kiss. It ended abruptly when the door behind them was suddenly flung open.

For a few seconds there was total silence. Then Joseph's voice rang out, smugly triumphant. 'Aha. We've done it, Nancy. And about time, too. We've finally found a man for Nina.'

Nina decided not to spoil her father's Christmas by pointing out that she'd found Fen all by herself.

THE END

PORTRAIT OF LOVE

Margaret McDonagh

Three generations of the Metcalfe family are settled and successful — professionally and personally. Or are they? An unexpected event sparks a chain reaction, bringing challenges to all the family. Loyalties are questioned, foundations rocked. A secret is exposed, unleashing a journey of discovery, combining past memories, present tensions, the promise of lost love and new hope for the future. Can the family embrace the events overtaking them? When the dust settles, will they emerge stronger and more united?

A BRIDE FOR JASON

Beverley Winter

Ace reporter Jason Edwards wants to marry Carly Smith, but Carly is a career girl and their families have been feuding for years. When she takes a job with Jason's family her aim is to safeguard her livelihood by exposing their unsavoury dealings. But Jason's instincts compel him to question her motives. Will the truth allow him to overcome the obstacles and still make Carly his bride? And when Carly discovers his reasons for doubting her, can she forgive him?

SNAPSHOTS FROM THE PAST

Angela Drake

When young widow Helen meets Ed her future at last seems bright. Her newfound happiness seems complete until a terrifying new shadow falls across her life. Someone is watching her, tracking her movements and sending her chilling photographs through the post — pictures relating to her past. Soon Helen can trust no one, and when her suspicions finally fall on Ed, their relationship is shattered. But who is Helen's tormentor? And will she and Ed ever get together again?

KISS AND TELL

Diney Delancey

When Ginny agreed to take her sister's place as au pair to two children on a skiing holiday in Austria, she wondered what she'd let herself in for. She'd been warned that Gareth Chilton, the children's uncle and guardian, was an arrogant — if good-looking — man, and was soon to experience his supremely overbearing manner! But Gareth's tender loving care for his niece and nephew melted Ginny's heart like snow in summer. And that was when her problems really began . . .